Sadie didn't say anything.

The only sound was the swish of the windshield wipers as he drove through the falling snow. He saw that he was headed for Helena. He knew he was waiting to hear from Crawford and simply driving to stay one step ahead of the men after them.

It didn't matter what town they reached as long as it had an airport, where he planned to put Sadie on a plane home. It had been a mistake calling her and getting her up here. He'd selfishly wanted her with him, he could admit now. He hadn't really needed her. He'd been right about one thing, though...it had been their last game. He'd almost gotten her killed for nothing.

"You know that I have to finish this."

Sadie said nothing for a few moments. "What exactly is this?"

"I thought I was just coming back here to pay off Grandville and free Keira from the debt and her no-account husband. Now I'm not sure what this is. All I know is I never should have gotten you involved."

This book is dedicated to my father, Harry Burton Johnson, who fed me lobster at fancy restaurants when things were going well—and free peanuts at a bar when they weren't. He taught me many of life's lessons and I'm sure that's why I'm a writer today. I had so much fun writing these characters because they were all close to my heart.

DEAD MAN'S HAND: A slang term used in poker for a two pair of black aces and black eights. The story goes that lawman and gambler "Wild Bill" Hickok was shot while holding the dead man's hand, which is why it's considered an unlucky two pair in poker today.

DEAD MAN'S HAND

New York Times Bestselling Author

B.J. DANIELS

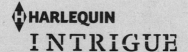

HARLEQUIN
INTRIGUE

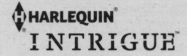

HARLEQUIN® INTRIGUE™

Recycling programs
for this product may
not exist in your area.

ISBN-13: 978-1-335-59120-3

Dead Man's Hand

Copyright © 2023 by Barbara Heinlein

Harlequin Enterprises ULC
22 Adelaide St. West, 41st Floor
Toronto, Ontario M5H 4E3, Canada
www.Harlequin.com

Printed in U.S.A.

B.J. Daniels is a *New York Times* and *USA TODAY* bestselling author. She wrote her first book after a career as an award-winning newspaper journalist and author of thirty-seven published short stories. She lives in Montana with her husband, Parker, and three springer spaniels. When not writing, she quilts, boats and plays tennis. Contact her at bjdaniels.com, on Facebook or on Twitter @bjdanielsauthor.

Books by B.J. Daniels

Harlequin Intrigue

A Colt Brothers Investigation

Murder Gone Cold
Sticking to Her Guns
Set Up in the City
Her Brand of Justice
Dead Man's Hand

Cardwell Ranch: Montana Legacy

Steel Resolve
Iron Will
Ambush before Sunrise
Double Action Deputy
Trouble in Big Timber
Cold Case at Cardwell Ranch

Visit the Author Profile page at Harlequin.com.

CAST OF CHARACTERS

DJ Diamond—Raised by a con man, he grew up expecting the worst—until he met Sadie and discovered he had a twin sister he knew nothing about.

Sadie Montclair—Raised by her godfather, the head of a criminal organization, all she wanted was a life like the wives' of the Colt brothers.

Buck Crawford—The PI must find his fiancée's missing twin brother before the wedding.

Ansley Brookshire—Her greatest desire is to have her twin brother walk her down the aisle.

Keira Diamond—Family meant something different to her than it did DJ.

Titus Grandville—The crooked banker who wants to destroy DJ Diamond.

Marcus Grandville—His son was about to destroy everything he'd built.

Chapter One

DJ Diamond shoved back his Stetson before glancing from the cards in his hand to the three men and one woman sitting around the table. After hours of poker, he felt as if he knew all of them better than their mothers did.

Except for the woman. She had a better poker face than any of the men. Also, she played her cards close to the vest—or in her case, the red halter top she wore. The top had the initials *AL* monogramed on it. Not her initials. He'd bet she picked up the garment at a garage sale. Her blond hair was long, pulled back into a ponytail that made her look like jailbait. All of it was at odds with her sharp honey-brown eyes and her skill at the game. All part of her act to throw grown men off their game.

It was working. The men had trouble keeping their eyes off her as she leaned forward to ante up—forcing their gazes away from the huge pot of money in the center of the table.

DJ could feel the tension in the room around him,

but he was as cool as a cucumber—as his uncle Charley used to say. He was aware of everything, though—including the exact amount of money in the pot as one of the men folded, but the other two stayed in, matching his bet, confident he was bluffing.

With luck, he'd be walking out with all the money—and the sexy young woman—before the night was over. And the night was almost over.

But right now, everyone was waiting on him.

He glanced down at his last five hundred dollars in chips for a moment, then picked them up and tossed them into the pile of money. "I'm going to have to sweeten the pot." Across the table, he saw the woman who called herself Tina shoot him a disbelieving look. He grinned and shrugged. "You want to see what I've got. It will cost you."

SADIE MONTCLAIR MUMBLED, "Arrogant fool," under her breath. She knew the Montana cowboy was planning on taking this pot and when he did all hell was going to break loose. She'd been reading the table since she sat down. The big doughy former football star next to her had a possible three queens. The guy in the expensive suit on the other side of her had to have had two pair, maybe even ace high. Luckily, the appliance salesman with the bad rug had folded. She'd marked him as the wild card of the group even before he'd started sweating profusely after losing so much money tonight.

She sighed as she looked at her jack-high straight with regret and tossed in her five Cs. Placing her cards facedown on the table, she leaned back, stretching, all eyes on her heaving chest.

"Let's see what you've got," the suit said, tossing his five hundred onto the pile of money and drawing the men's gazes again to the pot.

Sadie gave the arrogant fool across from her a shrug as she reached for the gun in her shoulder bag hanging off her chair. Her hand closed around the grip. She brought it out fast as the cowboy said, "Read 'em and weep," and fanned out his cards. An ace-high straight.

"You cheating bastard!" she yelled, kicking her chair back as she jumped to her feet. "Is it just him or were you all in on it?" she screamed as she waved the gun around.

The men were on their feet the moment they saw the gun in the hands of an angry woman, their chairs crashing to the floor behind them.

"You think you can cheat me, cowboy?" she yelled at him, wiping away his grin as she pulled the trigger.

The first report was deafening in the small dark room. Out of the corner of her eye, she saw the men scrambling for the door, the appliance salesman the slowest of the group. She fired twice more, putting three slugs into the arrogant fool cowboy's chest.

He fell backward, his chair crashing to the floor. She heard the others all rush out, the door slamming behind them before she stuffed the money into her shoulder bag, tossing the weapon in after it, and looked under the table. The Montana cowboy was lying sprawled on the floor, his Stetson beside him. "Arrogant fool."

Chapter Two

"I heard that," DJ Diamond said from the floor, and groaned. "Damn, Sadie. That hurt."

"That was pure arrogance to raise the bet again," she said. "You were just showing off. You can't keep pushing your luck—and mine."

He rose slowly, grimacing in pain as he tried to catch his breath. "Arrogant is shooting me three times. One wasn't good enough?"

"Three just felt right tonight," she said, cocking her hip as she watched him remove his shirt, then his body armor with the three slugs embedded in it.

"You must really hate me," he said, and grinned through his pain.

With his shirt off, it was hard not to admire the broad shoulders, the tapered waist or the vee of dark hair on the tanned chest that disappeared into his button-up jeans.

"What do you think?" he asked, raking a hand through his thick dark hair.

For a moment, she thought he was asking about

the way he looked. She blinked, realizing he was asking about their take tonight. "Not bad."

He laughed. "Come on, we made a haul. Maybe I pushed it a little, but it worked out. Don't forget the cards."

She had forgotten them, which would have been a mistake. If one of the gamblers realized they'd been had, he might come back here and find the marked deck. She scooped up the cards and added them to her shoulder bag. "I'm hungry."

DJ SHOOK HIS head as the shirt and body armor went into the satchel he'd brought with him. He pulled a fresh shirt out and put it on. "You're always hungry."

"I'm so hungry I could eat steak and lobster."

"That might be a problem dressed the way you are," he said as he settled his Stetson on that head of thick dark hair, then stepped to her and reached for the end of one thin strap that kept her halter top up.

She caught his hand. "You didn't get *that* lucky tonight." It was an old joke between partners whose relationship was strictly business. But more and more, she felt an undercurrent between them, one she suspected went both ways. Yet she never knew with DJ.

He chuckled, giving her that Diamond grin that apparently worked on women everywhere. "I do know a good barbecue place and I know how you feel about ribs." He grimaced as he touched his own ribs.

"Don't you think we should get rid of the loot first?"

"Couldn't I at least count it before we hand it over?" He flashed his baby blues.

"You don't need to count it and neither do I. We both know the take. You're stalling."

"Can you blame me? We should get hazardous pay for this."

"We should get into a new line of work," she said, knowing that he never would. He was a born poker player with larceny in his blood. "One of these days… In the meantime, let's get out of here. That one player made me nervous."

"There's always one who makes you nervous," he said as he put an arm around her and steered her toward the alternate exit door.

"The one that's going to get us both killed one day," she said under her breath.

His cell phone rang. He removed his arm from Sadie's shoulder to step away and take the call. "What's wrong, Keira?" She was sobbing, begging him to help her. He stepped farther away, never mixing business with family. "You have to stop crying so I can understand you."

She let out a cry and suddenly the voice on the phone was male. "I'll tell you what's wrong, Diamond. Your sister owes me money. A lot of money. Otherwise, we're going to have to sell her parts to the highest bidder."

"ONE OF YOUR GIRLFRIENDS?" Sadie asked as he caught up to her at her SUV in a parking garage blocks away from where they'd held the poker game. She'd left him to his phone call. Now, though, she noticed that his face was pinched, blue eyes flinty; his usual charm had vanished. Her first thought was that one of his women had called him to say she was pregnant. Then again it could be some angry husband threatening to kick his adorable ass. "You all right?"

"It's just something I need to take care of," he said, his voice tight. "Back in Montana. I'll be gone for a few days."

She went on alert. "You need help?"

"No, but thanks. Don't worry, I'll be back."

"Keep in touch," she said, and opened her car door. She saw him looking at her shoulder bag and shook her head. "You can't."

Nodding, he gave a shrug. "No, I can't. We had a deal. Don't worry, I'm sticking to it." He glanced around but she'd already made sure that the dark street was empty. As usual she wouldn't take the same route when she left, she would watch closely for a tail, she would take the usual precautions until tonight's take was locked up safe and secure.

Climbing behind the wheel, she closed the car door, but hesitated. She powered down the window. "DJ?" She'd noticed a tell she never saw at the poker table. He wasn't just nervous, he seemed…scared. "DJ, if—"

"I'm good. You take care."

"You, too," she said as she watched him walk, head down, toward his pickup parked even farther away. All her instincts told her he was in trouble. She reminded herself that he wasn't her responsibility. Theirs was a business partnership and nothing more. As long as they both stuck to the deal…

DJ SLID BEHIND the wheel of his pickup and rubbed a hand over his face. He'd tried to protect Keira from this life. He'd watched over her since the first time she'd shown up at the ranch—skinny, scraped up, hungry and scared. He suspected he'd probably arrived at the hardscrabble, rundown ranch in the same shape.

It wasn't much of a ranch, small by any standards. The only thing they raised was dust as criminals came and went. The place was straight out of an old Western movie set, a hideout where some came to recover from gunshot wounds. Others to cool their heels from the law. The ranch had been a dumping ground for lost souls. As the way of the ranch, no one asked questions. DJ and Keira had just been taken in like all the others, fed and clothed and conditioned to never know what to expect next.

Charley Diamond had been a small man with a hearty laugh and kind eyes. He was also a crook but with a code of the West. He helped those needing help—people like him down on their luck who always knew they had a place to recover. But he also took from the richer and pocketed the take.

When DJ had asked about his parents, Charley would rub the back of his neck and look up as if thinking. "Sorry, kid, I have no idea. You just arrived one day looking hungry and lost. Can't say who dropped you off. Doesn't matter. You're here now and I'm darned glad to have you. I could teach you a few things to help you survive for when you leave here."

DJ figured he'd been dropped off at the ranch just as Charley had said. He wondered, though, if his parents had promised to come back for him—and just hadn't. He also wondered if Charley knew more than he had told him. Not that worse things couldn't have happened to him—and to Keira. They both helped out around the ranch, earning their keep and becoming the only family either of them knew of—other than the man they called Uncle Charley.

When his uncle had fallen on hard times and lost the ranch, DJ was sixteen. Lucky for him, Charley had taught him the grift. Keira, who was six years younger, was too young for the road. She'd gone into foster care.

The next two years DJ spent staying one step ahead of the law and tough guys who wanted to kill him and his uncle. A born poker player, it didn't take DJ long though before he went out on his own way—eventually going legit since he found that he could make plenty of money without cheating.

He always kept in touch with Keira, made sure she had what she needed, and once she finished high school, paid for her college education and her wedding. Uncle Charley had given her away, even though like DJ, he didn't care for her choice of a husband. Luca Cross lacked ambition, while Keira wanted it all.

DJ suspected that Keira might be the reason her husband had gotten involved with gamblers and loan sharks. Now they were using her to collect what was owed. The same way DJ had ended up where he was now—owing the wrong people for all the wrong reasons.

He started the truck. Tonight he'd made thousands of dollars. But it was money he couldn't touch. He tried to look at it as work—the same way Sadie did. Some nights, though, he'd enjoyed it more than he should have. He felt only a little guilty since the men who'd gotten fleeced tonight had all been handpicked by a man they either owed or had crossed. The boss was a man who always collected debts—one way or another. Even though Uncle Charley was dead, DJ, now twenty-nine, was still paying off his uncle's last debts. It was the way it worked in this world. Some inherited wealth, others inherited debt. A man paid that debt.

Shifting into gear, DJ headed to his apartment to pack for the first flight he could get to Bozeman, Montana. From there Keira would pick him up. He had no idea what he would find when he got there, but that was nothing new. He'd spent his childhood expecting the worst.

Chapter Three

On her fiancé's ranch outside of Lonesome, Montana, Ansley Brookshire felt as if she couldn't breathe. Time was running out. Her longed-for Christmas wedding was days away. She was about to marry the man of her dreams. Just the thought stole her breath and made her heart pound with both excitement and anxiety.

It was all perfect except for one thing. Recently, she'd found out not only that she'd been adopted—but also that she had a twin brother. Now that she knew, she couldn't imagine getting married without him at the wedding. She had this image of him giving her away. Her heart ached for the two of them to be united and brought into the family that she'd only recently discovered.

Unfortunately, she had no idea where he was, even who he was. Like her, he'd been sold or given away right after birth by a woman who'd told their biological mother that they both had died. Ansley's adoptive mother had only wanted a baby girl and swore that she never even knew there had been another baby.

No one knew what had happened to her twin brother, since the woman who'd sold the babies was now dead. Ansley's fear was that like her, her twin might not even know he'd been adopted. She just hoped he'd gone to a good family and had a better childhood than hers. While she'd lived on an estate, never been deprived of anything money could buy, she'd been lonely and wished desperately for a family. All her childhood, she'd seen more of her nannies and the household staff than her parents.

When Ansley had learned that she was adopted, she'd gone in search of her biological mother. It had been like taking a stick to a hornet's nest. But she'd found her birth mother and the happy ending she'd hoped for. She wanted the same for her brother. Unfortunately, all leads had gone cold.

Her only hope was that the PIs at Colt Brothers Investigation would find him before it was too late. One of those PIs was her fiancé, Buck Crawford, who'd been working tirelessly for weeks searching for her missing twin. All they had to go on was the tiny bracelet his birth mother said she'd had made for him with the initials DJ on it for Del Junior. They couldn't even be sure that he'd ever gotten the bracelet.

"Maybe we should postpone the wedding," Buck had said, but she hadn't had the heart to do that. They both wanted to be married soon. She told herself she was being too sentimental. A Christmas wedding was her dream and Buck was everything she'd ever wanted in a husband.

"No," she'd told him. "We're getting married. Anyway, I still have hope that we'll find DJ before the wedding."

Now the wedding was looming and still no leads on her twin.

"Ansley?" a female voice called. "Or should I call you DelRae?"

She hadn't heard a vehicle in the deep snow, but now she heard the front door close. Footfalls headed her way. She had to smile, wondering at twenty-nine years old if she would ever answer to the name her birth mother had given her. Or if she should even bother trying.

"In here," she called back to Bella Colt, a sister-in-law. Along with finding her birth mother, she'd also found her biological father's family—the Colt brothers of Colt Brothers Investigation and their wives. She now had four half brothers, Tommy, Davy, James and Willie, and their wives, Bella, Carla, Lori and Ellie. She'd instantly felt a part of the family.

On top of that, she'd also fallen in love with the brothers' best friend, Buck Crawford, a fellow PI at the agency.

Bella came into the living room where Ansley had been wrapping Christmas presents. "What in the world! Did you buy out all the stores in Missoula?"

She shook her head sheepishly. "I've never had a family to buy for before. My adoptive mother bought her own Christmas presents for me to wrap. My adoptive father had his secretary pick up something for each of us. He usually also had the secretary return anything Maribelle or I got for him, saying he didn't need anything. So shopping for all of you has been so much fun. Don't tell anyone, but I started shopping even before Thanksgiving. I couldn't wait."

"You really are too much." Bella hugged her awkwardly around the baby. James's wife Lori had given birth to two identical baby boys a few months ago.

Ansley motioned her friend into the kitchen. "Coffee?"

"I shouldn't." Bella lumbered in, both hands over her protruding stomach. "Water tastes so…watery," she groaned.

"Eggnog?"

"Don't tempt me," her friend said, and held her side for a moment. "They've been kicking like crazy. I suspect they've got my and Tommy's worst traits," she said with a laugh as she took a chair and the glass of eggnog. "It would be just like them to decide to be born in the middle of your wedding." All four Colt wives were her bridesmaids, with their husbands the groomsmen.

A silence fell between them as Ansley poured herself a cup of coffee and joined Bella at the table.

"Are you sure you don't want to wait?" Bella asked. "Even if Buck manages to find him, he'll be a complete stranger. Do you really want a stranger standing up with you at your wedding?"

Ansley laughed. "He won't be a stranger. I know him—that is, I feel like I do. He's my *twin*. He won't be a stranger."

Bella looked skeptical but let it go. "What if Buck doesn't find him before the wedding?"

"Then we go ahead anyway," she said, knowing how disappointed she would be.

"You could just postpone it," Bella suggested.

It wasn't like she hadn't thought about postponing the wedding. "Wait for how long, though? What if DJ's never found? Buck and I can't wait. We love each other. We want to get married." She sighed. "But at the same time, how can I start my life not knowing where my twin is, how he is or even if he's still alive? I've always felt as if there was a missing piece of me. Then I found you and the Colt brothers and Buck."

"And still something was missing," Bella said.

She nodded. "Once I found out that I had a twin who my mother called DJ for Del Junior, I knew I had to find him." She swallowed the lump in her throat. "Even if he can't be found by the wedding, we will find him. Buck won't stop looking for him."

"Neither will the Colt brothers. They were shocked to find they had a half sister. Imagine their reaction to meeting a half brother. If he is anything like you, we are going to love him. We'll love him anyway," she said with a laugh and took a sip of her eggnog. "So, is it going to be Ansley or DelRae? Or are you going to answer to both?"

"I have no sentimental ties to the Ansley name or the Brookshire name. I love DelRae, I'm just not sure I'll ever remember to answer to it."

"I can understand that you might want to ditch your first name and last with both Maribelle and Harrison Brookshire headed for prison. But you also can't erase your past," Bella said. "You know my father almost went to prison at one point." She shook her head. "A long story for another time," she said, awkwardly getting to her feet. "I have some last-minute Christmas shopping to do, but I wanted to check on you."

She rose to show her out. She couldn't believe how close she'd gotten to her new family and in record time. She hoped the same would be true for her twin when he was found.

At the door, Bella turned to take her hand and squeeze it. "Don't give up hope. There's still time."

All she could do was nod and smile her thanks even as she felt sick with worry that time was running out. Worse, the news might not be good. Her twin might not have survived. Or he might want nothing to do with her and the rest of the family.

BUCK CRAWFORD DISCONNECTED and leaned back, feeling more positive than he had in weeks. "I think I might have found a lead," he said, leaving his office to walk out into the main reception area of Colt Brothers Investigation.

James looked up from his father's old desk expectantly. The brothers had all done their best to find Ansley's twin brother before hitting a brick wall and being forced to move on to other clients. Buck was determined to continue looking for the missing twin right up until the wedding.

"It's an old friend of Judy Ramsey's who moved away after her house burned down." Buck remembered the vacant lot next to Judy's house. "Luella Lindley lived there and knew Judy during the time frame when Ansley and her brother were born. I'm hoping she's going to be able to help."

"For Ansley's sake, I hope so." He smiled. "Yours, too, since I know how badly you want to marry my sister. But what if you don't find him? Would you postpone the wedding?"

Buck shook his head. "I hope not, but Ansley has her heart set on her twin giving her away. Not that I blame her. I can't imagine what it's like to find out you have a twin brother you never knew existed. I'd want to find him, too."

"Let's hope she gets her happy ending. I just worry. Ansley lucked out. Even though the Brookshires weren't the family she'd hoped for, she had what most people would consider a good life. Then she got all of us." He grinned. "But it could have turned out a lot worse for her brother."

Admittedly, Buck worried about that as well. Ansley needed a happy ending and that meant finding her twin. Hopefully before the wedding. He didn't want to think about postponing the wedding. He wanted Ansley for his wife now. The waiting was killing him. He was anxious to start their lives together.

But until Del Jr. was found, dead or alive, he knew Ansley would be heartbroken. That was something Buck couldn't stand. He'd do anything to make her happy.

Buck couldn't help but think about all that Ansley had gone through to find her birth mother. It had been dangerous. People had died, others had gone to prison. Both Buck and Ansley were lucky to be alive. He really hoped that wouldn't be the case finding her twin.

"Let's hope Luella Lindley has the answers we need," he told James. "I'm driving down to Casper, Wyoming, to talk to her in person. Don't mention this to Ansley. I don't want to get her hopes up."

Buck knew it was more than that. He didn't want to give her bad news with their wedding and first Christmas together just over a week away.

"CAN YOU TURN that off?" DJ asked after he and Keira were headed north away from the busiest airport in the state, Yellowstone International just outside of Bozeman, Montana. He wanted to put all this progress in the rearview mirror as they headed toward the mountains.

She reached over and turned off the radio and the Christmas music. DJ realized he'd lost track of not just weeks, but months. How could it already be this close to Christmas? It wasn't as if he celebrated the holiday. He had no warm and fuzzy family holiday memories. In fact, he was always glad once the season was over—not that it wasn't a good time financially for him and Sadie. The kind of people they dealt with were more reckless with their money this time of year, some out of Christmas cheer, most out of greed or desperation.

"Tell me what's going on," he said once they were on the open highway.

Keira's hands gripped the wheel seemingly tighter, her eyes galvanized on the road ahead as she chewed nervously at her lower lip. "I don't want you to get mad." Too late for that. "It was a mistake. He didn't know."

DJ swore. Of course Luca knew. No one gambled without knowing they might lose—and they might lose big if they didn't stop. "How much?"

"Seventy-five large originally," she said without looking at him. "I didn't know that he'd borrowed more to keep up with the interest payments."

He never lost his temper. It was bad for business. But right now...

"I wouldn't have called you, but..."

But there was no one else.

She concentrated on the road.

He chose his words carefully, determined not to take his frustration and anger out on her. "When you're involved with these kinds of people you don't go to another one and borrow more. That's a good way to end up in a ditch dead. Or in your case sold to the highest bidder. Who are these men your husband got involved with?"

"Do you remember Titus Grandville? He's an investment banker in the same building as his father's bank."

Is that what he was calling himself? "Crooks wear suits, too, baby sister," he said, and turned to stare out at the passing countryside while he tamped down his anger and tried to concentrate on the beauty. It had been so long since he'd been back here. He'd forgotten how breathtaking the snowcapped mountains were. The pines were so dark green against the cobalt blue of the big sky. He felt an old childhood ache for a place that he'd once thought of as paradise.

"Who's his muscle?" he finally asked.

She mugged a distasteful face. "Butch Lamar. He's the one you talked to on the phone. He's new in town. Hangs out on the Turner Ranch. He's friends with Rafe Westfall, the son of one of the men who used to live out at our old ranch." She shot him a look. "They're serious, DJ. The first time Luca couldn't pay, they beat him up real bad. This last time…"

"He still alive?" DJ asked, hoping so for selfish reasons.

"Barely. He's hiding out. That's why they grabbed me."

"Did you know?" he had to ask. Her silence said it all. He swore and turned on her. "You grew up with this. How could you let him?"

"*I didn't let him*. He thought he was—"

"Smarter, right?" DJ cursed under his breath. "And he thought he was going to surprise you, make you happy. How do I know this is the last time he's going to have to be bailed out?" He saw her jaw tighten.

"I'm divorcing him. I'm done. He's on his own after this."

He studied her, trying to decide if she was telling the truth or just saying what he wanted to hear. He made a living reading people, but his little sister was a mystery to him because he loved her so much. "Does he know that?"

"Yes. He says he was trying to make money to save our marriage."

"Bull," DJ snapped.

She swung her head in his direction. "Don't you think I know that?" She quickly turned back to her driving as the SUV swerved. "It's not the first time. We had to sell everything last time."

He found himself grinding his teeth and had to look out the side window again. In his line of work, temper was a real weakness and one he couldn't afford. But this wasn't business. This was personal.

Ahead, he saw the turnoff to Whitehall. "Take this exit. We'll get a couple of rooms here and go into Butte in the morning." What he didn't say was that he wasn't ready to go back. Not yet. The city brought back too many memories.

"By the way, where is Luca hiding out?" He asked it casually, but Keira knew him too well.

"I don't want you to do anything to him."

He waited, counting off the seconds until she finally spoke as if she knew he'd find out even if she refused to tell him.

"Lonesome. It's a small town up by—"

"I know where it is," DJ said. "Why'd he choose it?"

She didn't answer right away. "He's staying at Uncle Charley's cabin up there."

Charley had a cabin? This was news. He thought that his uncle had lost everything back when he lost the ranch. And why outside of Lonesome, one of only a few small Montana towns that he noticed his uncle had avoided? When asked, Charley had been surprised that he'd noticed. "Some towns aren't worth the trouble." But he'd looked at him strangely, as if he wanted to say more but had changed his mind.

DJ had guessed that Charley had unfinished business in Lonesome. Those last few years of his uncle's life, he hadn't seen much of him. When he did see him, he worried that Charley was in more trouble than he could dig himself out of. As it turned out, that was true.

Charley always had his secrets. Now he knew that his uncle had a cabin that he'd somehow managed to keep—and Keira knew about it.

He glanced over at her, wondering what other secrets they'd both kept from him.

Chapter Four

Leaving Keira in Whitehall, DJ rented an SUV and drove to Butte alone. He found the investment banker's office on the top floor of the Grandville Building. He'd checked it out online last night as he prepared for this. A four-story brick edifice from the late eighteen hundreds that housed the Grandville Bank started by Titus's great-grandfather. The bank was still on the ground floor with two upper floors converted into condos and the top floor office space.

He found Titus Grandville in his corner office overlooking the historical section of downtown Butte. "Nice digs," DJ said as the banker motioned for him to take one of the leather club chairs. He declined and approached the man in the large office chair behind the massive desk.

Like all the Grandvilles, Titus was short and squat with a cowlick at the crown of his brown hair. While dressed like a respectable investment banker, he still looked like the thug he was.

"Let me understand the problem here," DJ said

quietly, calmly. "You came after my sister to threaten her over debts run up by the deadbeat husband she is divorcing. Is that right?"

Titus narrowed dark eyes that were a little too close together. He dropped his hand below the desk. To buzz for security if needed? Or reach for a weapon? "I hope we can settle this like respectable gentlemen."

DJ laughed. "We'd have to be respectable gentlemen." He lowered his voice. "You need to leave Keira alone. What is it going to take?"

The banker smiled and leaned back in his large office chair, steepling his fingers on his round middle. Apparently, mentioning money made Titus less nervous. "Someone has to pay what's owed."

Grandville was enjoying this a little too much. He remembered him as a kid. To say there was bad blood between them was putting it mildly. Titus had always lorded it over him. Not that everyone in Butte hadn't known that Titus was a Grandville. Who knew what DJ was?

Just the sight of his smug face was enough to make him want to leap over the massive desk and take the man by the throat. But it wouldn't solve the problem. DJ had known the moment he heard Keira crying on the phone that he was going to have to come up here and pay them off. The very idea stuck in his craw because of his dislike for the Grandvilles.

"Settle for twenty-five."

Titus shook his head. "Seventy-five with interest on the loan adding up every day—"

"Fifty thousand and I don't throw you out that big window behind you," DJ said.

"Diamond, you have always been a loose cannon." Titus tsked. "All right. For old time's sake, seventy-five and no more interest as long as this is handled quickly. By the end of the week."

"And you never go near my sister again."

The banker nodded, but DJ didn't feel as if this was settled. "Do I need to say it? You never do business with Luca Cross again either."

"Why do you care about him?" Titus asked, sounding amused.

DJ didn't answer, afraid to voice his fear that Keira wouldn't leave the man because she still loved him. Love was a fickle, foolish sentiment, one he avoided when it came to women. Family was another story, though, maybe especially family you didn't share blood with.

"I'll get your money. But you do realize that I'm going to have to put together a poker game to make it happen. That all right with you?"

Titus rocked forward in his chair, taking the bait quicker than DJ had expected. "I could suggest a couple of players with deep pockets I'd like to see cleaned. Let me know when and where."

"You're welcome to come play as well," DJ said with a grin.

The banker laughed. "I'm smarter than that. And Diamond? I'll need that money by the end of the week."

As he turned to leave, the banker called after him, "So it's true. You're paying off your uncle's debts, too." Definite amusement in his voice.

DJ didn't trust himself to look back. If he saw that self-righteous look on Titus's face, he might just make good on his earlier threat.

As he left the building, he quit kidding himself that there was another way to solve this. He was going to have to pay, one way or another. He had the money in his savings account. Seventy-five grand wouldn't even make a dent. He could pay Titus off and walk away, but the very thought turned his stomach. He'd told Keira to stay put in Whitehall until this was settled. She'd be safe there—as long as she didn't do anything foolish like try to go to her husband.

DJ stopped for a moment as he tried to talk himself out of the plan that had come together the moment he'd walked into Grandville's office and seen Titus sitting behind his big desk. His good sense advised him to just pay the debt and forget it. Unfortunately, it wasn't just about the money. It hardly ever was.

He made the call to the one person he needed right now. "Sadie?" He hated the way his voice almost broke. It made him admit how much he wanted her help, as if a part of him worried that he couldn't do this without her, and that alone should have scared him. He'd come to depend on her. But even as he thought it, he knew it was a hell of a lot more than that. "I need you."

"I wondered how long it would take before you realized that," she joked.

"It's my sister. Her bad-choice soon-to-be hope-fully ex-husband's fault. He's taken off and left her holding the bag."

"How heavy is this bag?"

"Seventy-five large."

"I can be on the next plane. Where am I headed?"

DJ closed his eyes for a moment, relief and some-thing much stronger making his knees weak. "I'll pick you up at the airport outside of Bozeman. I'll be the cowboy in the hat," he said, needing to lighten the moment for fear he'd say something he couldn't take back. "I really appreciate this," he said, his voice rough with emotion. "Thank you."

"No problem, partner. I'm on my way."

SADIE DISCONNECTED, a lump in her throat. *DJ had a sister?* Why had she thought it was just him and the conman uncle who'd raised him? Not that DJ knew any more about her life than she did his. When they'd been thrown together, she'd just assumed that he was like her, from the same background, caught up in a world not to either of their making or liking. DJ had taken on his uncle's debt to the organization her godfather ran. The payments on that debt, which were almost paid, were what had kept them together.

She'd done her best to treat it like business, especially after her godfather had warned her against getting too close to DJ Diamond. But she'd gotten to know the man from sitting across a poker table from him all that time.

While she'd been shocked to learn that DJ had a little sister, she wasn't surprised that he would drop everything to bail her out. What worried her was that she'd never heard him sound like he had on the phone. Desperate? Anxious? Neither was good in this business, she thought as she quickly threw some clothing and money into a bag along with their decks of marked cards.

Two hours later, as she boarded a plane to Montana, she reminded herself that this might be the last time she saw DJ. Their "arrangement" was over. She'd told her godfather that she wanted out as soon as DJ's debt was paid. He'd been disappointed but not surprised.

"What will you do? You'll miss this," he'd said.

"I don't think so. I want a family." She didn't have to tell him that she also wanted to be as far away from criminal organizations as she could get.

"I understand," he'd said. "Your father was like that. Tell Diamond we're even. His uncle's debt is paid in full. My present to you since I can tell that you have a soft spot for him."

Sadie had only smiled. "Thank you."

"But you're not quitting because of him, right?"

"No, that partnership will be over," she said, hating how hard it would be to walk away from DJ Diamond. She'd grown more than fond of him. But she would walk away, she'd told herself.

"Good," her godfather said. "By the way, you're better at this than your father ever was, and he was pretty darned good." It had been her father who'd taught her that poker wasn't a game of chance. It was a game of skill, mental toughness and endurance.

"Never sit down at a table unless you know you can beat everyone there—one way or another," he'd said over and over. "You're going to lose sometimes, so never throw good money after bad. It all comes down to reading your opponents and knowing when to cash in and walk away."

Whatever DJ had going on in Montana, it was time to cash in and walk away. She would tell DJ when she got to Montana. She would also offer him the seventy-five grand so they wouldn't have to use the cards in her carry-on bag. He wouldn't take it, but she would offer. She feared that unlike her, he'd never be able to step away from the con. He enjoyed it too much. But eventually, his luck would run out. The thought made her sad. As her godfather had said, she had grown a soft spot for the cowboy.

BUCK CRAWFORD MADE the drive down to Casper, Wyoming, arriving in late afternoon. Luella Lindley lived in a small house in the older part of town. She was in her sixties, retired after being a telephone operator for years. She lived alone except for her three cats, George, Bob and Ingrid. She had a weakness for chocolate, her husband had been dead for almost twenty years, and she played bingo on Tuesday nights at the Senior Center.

He'd gotten all that information the first time he'd talked to her. Had she known Judy Ramsey? Yes. "We were like two peas in a pod," Luella had told him. "Sisters, that's what Judy called us, me being the older sister."

It took a good five minutes after ringing the doorbell for the woman to answer the door. She'd warned him that she used a walker and would be slow. Luella opened the door, leaning on her walker and smiling broadly. The smell of meat loaf wafted out, making his stomach growl.

"I hope you're hungry," she said, her blue eyes sparkling with excitement, giving him the feeling that she didn't get many visitors. "I made my famous meat loaf. Come on in. No need to stand out there on the front step." She turned and led the way into the house. "Have a seat." She went from the walker to a recliner. "Didn't expect a good-looking cowboy, although you did sound young on the phone. Are you really a private detective?"

"Yes, and you should have demanded proof of identification before you let me in," he said.

She laughed. "I saw you drive up. You didn't look that dangerous."

Buck knew he couldn't leave until he had meat loaf, so he let Luella talk about everything under the sun for a few minutes before he said, "What can you tell me about Judy Ramsey?"

"Sweet thing she was. Never had a lick of sense when it came to men, though," Luella said with a shake of her head. "Broke my heart every time she let some man hurt her."

"You knew her twenty-nine years ago. Did she tell you she was pregnant?"

The elderly woman nodded. "She was scared, but I could tell a part of her liked the idea of being a mother." She shook her head. "Turned out it was female problems. No baby. Never going to have one. By then, she'd realized she wasn't mother material."

"Did she tell you about meeting Maribelle Brookshire?"

"Read all about it in the paper. I have the Lonesome paper sent to me. The news is old by the time it arrives, but I don't care. It doesn't cost much and that is my hometown."

"So she told you about her deal with Maribelle to buy the baby if it was a girl?"

"No," she said after a moment. "I could tell something was going on, but no. She was devastated when she found out there was no baby. I didn't realize the main reason was because she'd already sold the baby to Maribelle Brookshire. I thought her behavior was due to a man, but then she began asking questions about babies… I had to wonder why since I knew she wasn't having any of her own."

"What kind of questions?"

"Like what they ate, how to burp them, how to even put on a diaper and what you needed to buy for a baby. I thought she'd gone crazy."

"If you've read the news, then you know that Maribelle and Harrison Brookshire are awaiting trial for Judy's death. I'm engaged to their daughter they bought from Judy, Ansley Brookshire."

"My goodness, isn't that wonderful. That poor child needs a happy ending. Those so-called parents of hers, they deserve the electric chair for what they did to her, not to mention poor Judy."

"Ansley had a twin brother. Do you have any idea what Judy might have done with him?"

Luella shook her head. "I can understand why she did what she did. I mean, that's how we became such good friends—her moving in next door to me. She couldn't have done that without the money she got from that woman. Not that I approve of her means."

"Is it possible she gave the baby boy to someone she knew in Lonesome? I would think that she would have taken him to someone she trusted, someone with knowledge as to how to care for an infant."

The woman nodded sagely. "You're thinking me."

"The birth mother wasn't in any shape to take care of the baby. Also she thought both babies had died. So Judy had to have taken the baby boy to a friend."

Luella seemed to squirm a little in her seat. "Is talking to you like talking to a lawyer, anything I say is just between us?"

Buck hesitated, but only for a moment. "I just want

to find him. I don't want to get anyone in trouble, especially you."

"That didn't quite answer my question."

"She brought you the baby, didn't she?"

Chapter Five

DJ had never been happier to see anyone. He stared at Sadie as she came down the stairs at the Yellowstone International Airport—his second time there in days. He blinked realizing he'd never seen her in normal clothes. Today, she wore designer jeans, a pale blue cashmere sweater and furry snow boots. She had her sheepskin coat thrown over one shoulder, her leather shoulder bag on the other and the expensive carry-on in her hand.

She looked like a million bucks. Everything fit like a glove, and she fit in here in the Gallatin Valley where the wealthy came to find paradise. She could have passed for any one of them because, he realized with a start, she was one of them. Sometimes he forgot that she'd been raised in Palm Beach, rubbing elbows with the rich and powerful.

He knew he wasn't the only man staring at this breathtaking woman with her long blond hair resting around her shoulders. But when those honey-brown eyes found him, he felt like the only man in the world. She smiled, reminding him how amazing she was—and how unattainable.

His partner, Sadie Montclair, the smartest, funniest, sexiest woman he'd ever met, was off-limits in a big life-threatening way. Even if her godfather hadn't threatened him if he even thought about seducing her, DJ knew that she wouldn't look twice at someone like him. Not seriously, anyway.

"How was your flight?" he asked as he took her carry-on and led her outside into the cold, snowy December day to his rental SUV. "Thanks again for coming. You fly over so many mountains to get here. Sometimes the turbulence can get to you, but the view can be pretty spectacular."

"Are you really trying to make small talk, DJ Diamond?" she asked with a laugh as he climbed behind the wheel. She could tell he was nervous. He saw a flicker of concern in her gaze before she said, "Tell me about the people your sister owes this money to."

So like Sadie to get right to business. He tried to calm his nerves, having second thoughts about getting her involved in this. But while he kept thinking that he shouldn't have called her and she shouldn't have come, he was so glad that she was here. Maybe this was a mistake, but right now he couldn't help feeling relieved. Sadie balanced him; it's why they were such a good team.

He started the engine, stopped at the booth to turn in his parking ticket and drove out of the airport onto Interstate 90 headed west, mentally kicking himself for getting her involved in his family mess. "I shouldn't have called you."

"Of course you should have. If I hadn't wanted to come, I wouldn't have. I'm here for you. We're partners. It's just that you were acting like you'd picked up your girlfriend at the airport."

He nodded, swallowed and tried to relax. She was right. He wasn't himself around this version of Sadie. But he better pull it together. He cleared this throat and turned to business. "The men? Old money. Suits, ties, hired muscle. Grandville is a cocky bastard. Would they kill Keira? Probably not. Would they mess her up? Yeah."

SADIE SAW THAT her words had hurt DJ. But she'd seen the way he looked at her as she'd come down the stairs at the terminal. It was going to be hard enough to walk away from this partnership as it was. She couldn't have him looking at her like that. Worse, she couldn't feel like she *was* his girlfriend he was picking up at the airport.

"Doesn't sound like anything we haven't dealt with before," she said as she took in the scenery as he drove, reminding herself that this was just another job.

She'd never been to Montana, but she could see the appeal. There was a winter wonderland outside her window. Everything was frosted with snow from the mountains to the pine trees, from houses to the fence posts they passed. Even the air seemed to sparkle with snow crystals. She couldn't help being enchanted as she saw a red barn with Christmas lights in the shape of a star on the side.

"I thought we'd make a big haul, pay off Grandville and get out," DJ was saying. "He's supplying at least one of the players, someone's pockets he wants us to pick. I'll find someone to front the game who can bring in a local hard hitter or two to the mix."

"Whatever you think is best," she said as she saw a snowman in one of the yards. "Montana really is like the photographs I've seen. It's beautiful."

He glanced over at her. "You should see it in the spring. That's my favorite time of year, when everything greens up after a long, dull, colorless winter."

"I'd like that," she said. "I was thinking on the way up here. I have seventy-five thousand that I could—"

"Not a chance," he said quickly.

"It's my money, nothing to do with my godfather, and I wouldn't—"

"No," he said, shaking his head. "Thanks, but no. If you don't want to do this, just say so. No harm, no foul."

"I told you. I'm here. I'll do it. I just thought…" She could see that she'd offended him. "Sorry."

He shook his head. "I can't take your money."

"I get it." Sadie considered him for a moment. DJ saved what money he made when gaming legally. He was a hell of a poker player. She was betting that he had a whole lot more than seventy-five grand lying around. So if he wanted to, he could pay off his sister's creditor. This wasn't so much about money, she suspected. This was about getting even. With this Grandville he mentioned?

"Want to tell me what you have planned?"

"Just a friendly game of poker." He grinned as he looked over at her. She knew that look. He loved this. "I'm keeping you under wraps. Butte's an old mining town. I've got you a room at a local historic hotel that's been completely renovated. It's fancy—just like you. Room service, a bar, order whatever you want, any clothes you need."

"Sounds like you've thought of everything. So I'm the mark," she said, and shook her head in amusement. "A new role, huh?"

"One that clearly you were born into," he said, his gaze taking her in again.

She tried not to read too much into the look. She knew DJ. He couldn't help the charm. The man had an appreciation for women. All women—she couldn't let herself forget that.

Sadie told herself that this was just going to be another poker game like so many others they'd played together. She knew the drill. The two of them had it down pat. But as she studied him while he drove, she had to ask, "You sure about this? Once things get personal—"

"Like your godfather says, otherwise it is only money."

"Don't kid yourself. He likes the money just as much as the retribution."

They drove in silence for a few minutes. "It will

be our last time." DJ tapped on the steering wheel, seeming lost in thought. "I know we're close to paying my uncle's debt. However much he owes for interest, I'll pay it from my own money. I'm done." He glanced at her as if to see how she was taking the news.

She nodded. "Talk about like minds. I was going to tell you the same thing. My godfather says you're paid in full." He turned to give her a suspicious look. "I had nothing to do with it. He says it's time."

DJ turned back to his driving and chewed on that for a while. She was wondering if he would miss it. If he would miss her. "One last big score." When she said nothing, he asked, "You're really up for this?"

"We're a team. If this is our last time…I wouldn't want to miss it for anything."

His gaze locked with hers for a few earth-shaking moments. She felt heat rush to her cheeks and quickly turned away. Was this really their last game? Her heart ached at the thought of never seeing DJ again as she watched the snowy landscape blur past her side window. Probably for the best, she thought, because she seemed to be losing her resistance to his charm. She couldn't let down her guard now when it was almost over. She knew how DJ was with women. She didn't want to be one of them.

It surprised her, though, that he'd been ready to end their relationship, even if it had been all business. Maybe like her, he'd decided it was time. Yet it made her uneasy, as if he was worried this was their last game for another reason. Just how dangerous was this going to be?

"You can still walk away," he said as if reading her mind.

He had to know her better than that. "Have I ever let you down?" she asked, still not looking at him.

"Never."

She heard something in his voice, an emotion she hadn't heard before. But by the time she dared look over at him, all his attention was back on the highway ahead.

BUCK HELD HIS BREATH. This was the first decent lead he'd had on finding the missing twin. He couldn't help but think of Ansley. He had to find the last missing piece of her. She'd risked her life to find her birth mother, who had been told that both babies died.

"Can I go to prison for this?" Luella asked, her voice cracking.

"You aren't going to prison," he said. "Unless you harmed the baby."

"Oh, good Lord, no," she said, sounding shocked. "I'd never hurt a precious baby. He was so sweet, so tiny, so precious. I didn't care where Judy had gotten him. I should have. I know that was wrong. I just wanted to help her. She was beside herself, afraid he wasn't going to make it. I assured her I could help."

He saw her hesitate and suspected he knew where she was headed. "You knew someone who could take care of the baby."

"I'm not saying who, but yes. We took him over there and my…friend who'd just given birth six months before was still breastfeeding. He took right to it like the little champ he was and perked right up."

Buck thought how easy it would be to find out if Luella had a daughter or daughter-in-law who'd given birth that year—but only if it came to that. "So you left the baby with her?"

"Only for a few days. I still didn't know where Judy had gotten the little darling. Had I been younger, I would have kept him. I wanted to, but there would have been talk. Lonesome is a small town." She shook her head. "It wasn't possible. But it was so hard to give him back."

"Back to Judy?"

She nodded. "She knew someone who wanted a baby." Luella began shaking her head even before he asked who. "I didn't want to know. I'd involved people I cared about already. I knew not to push it."

He tried to hide his disappointment. "You must have some idea. You were Judy's best friend. You knew some of the same people."

She looked away for a moment and he felt hope resurface.

As DJ TURNED off the interstate and headed toward uptown Butte, Sadie took in the city sprawled across the side of the mountain—except for the right side, where much of the mountain was missing. "They still mine here?" she asked in surprise.

"Butte is a hard-core mining town," DJ said. "It started as a mining camp back in the 1860s and quickly grew to become Montana's first industrial city." They passed large abandoned old brick buildings, the windows either missing or covered in dust. "It's fallen on hard times since then, but the Continental pit is still active as an open-pit copper and molybdenum mining operation. Mining still pays better than any other industry in the state."

"Which is why we're here," Sadie said. "Aren't miners…a bit rough to deal with if things go south, though?"

"We aren't taking the miners' money. We're after the people above them who make the big money."

She was relieved to hear that. With her godfather, he handpicked the players in the games she and DJ relieved of their cash. Even so, there were some who often made her nervous. She'd learned that you could never tell what a person might do—especially if you'd just spent hours taking his money.

DJ headed up the mountainside, passing more old brick buildings in what was obviously the historic district. She couldn't help being fascinated just thinking of the history here as he pulled down an alley behind a large old brick hotel. The sign on the top floor read Hotel Finlen.

Sadie shot him a look as he stopped at the hotel's service entrance off the alley, but he didn't seem to notice. "Butte has an amazing history—and so does this hotel. Charles Lindbergh, Harry S. Truman and even JFK visited the Finlen," he said with an enthusiasm that was catching. "I love this hotel and this town. Butte was once the largest city between Chicago and San Francisco. You'll like this place. The Finlen was architecturally inspired by the Hotel Astor in New York and was built to impress in 1924."

She couldn't help smiling at him. Clearly this old mining town meant a lot to him. "How do you know all this?" she asked, hoping he would talk about his childhood here.

"The Finlen was my uncle's favorite hotel. He often paid the bill so we could come back. That wasn't true of most other hotels we stayed in."

She laughed. "Do you always use the back door off the alley?"

"Used to a lot. But today?" He shrugged. "I know people here." Of course he did. He knew people all over Montana and the northwest after growing up with a conman uncle. Not that DJ had ever offered anything about himself or his past. Just as she hadn't. But her godfather had told her a few things about the man before he'd asked her to work with him.

"I want to keep our partnership quiet. I hate to ask you to walk around to the front of the building through the snow and slush, but we can't be connected," DJ said. "I need you to hang out here for a day or so. Like I said, buy expensive meals, shop, whatever. Throw money around. I'll contact you when I'm ready, but for this one you're a high roller."

"I think I'm going to enjoy being the mark,"

she said as he reached into the glove box and took out a thick envelope of money. She waved it away. "Thanks, but no. You don't get to be the only one to take the high road."

He looked as if he wanted to argue, before stuffing the envelope into his inside jacket pocket. "You'll get every penny back." He pointed up the street behind them. "It's easier to go that way. In this part of the older city, the streets and sidewalks are steep since they built the original city on the side of a mountain. I know how steep because I was the one who had to make the run for it so the employees chased me—and not my uncle."

His words hit her at heart level. She knew he'd had a rough childhood, but she hadn't known any details and now didn't know what to say. A cold silence seemed to surround the cab of the pickup for a moment. "It was a game for me," he said as if seeing her sympathy even though she tried hard to hide it. He grinned. "When we were flush, we ate lobster tail and steak from china plates on white linen tablecloths with real silver at the best places in town. True, when we were between scores, we ate whatever I could scrounge up—often from food trays left out in hotel hallways. But you'd be amazed what people leave. Like I said, as a kid it was a game. A scavenger hunt." He shrugged and she could tell that he wished he hadn't told her any of this. So why had he?

"Bet you could run fast." She smiled even though she felt more like crying as she thought about DJ as a boy outrunning hotel employees so his uncle didn't have to. "I can't wait to see this hotel that meant so much to you and your uncle." She met his gaze. "I like seeing this place through your eyes. Thanks for sharing. And don't worry about me. I'll do my part."

"I never doubt it. Thanks again, Sadie."

She hesitated, surprised how much she wanted to reassure him. He seemed so vulnerable here in this place that had been such an important part of his younger life.

But she was the one who'd kept their relationship strictly business. While she couldn't *not* have regrets, it was almost over. The thought made a lump rise in her throat as she climbed out, closed the door and headed back down the alley. As she walked she couldn't help comparing his life to her own. Hers had been a fairy-tale princess's existence compared to his. There was no way she couldn't help him get the money for his sister. But she still felt uneasy. She didn't know this place or these people. Nor did she and DJ have the protection of her godfather. They were on their own.

At the front of the hotel, she pushed open the door, lifted her chin and strode in as if she owned the place. It was time to go to work.

Chapter Six

Buck watched Luella turn away to rinse out a cup in the sink. Stalling. He held his tongue although it was killing him. He could tell that she knew something he desperately needed. He thought of Ansley, his love for her, their upcoming wedding. *Please.*

"I honestly don't know for certain," Luella said. "I swear."

"I believe you, Luella," Buck said. "But anything you can tell me will help. My fiancée is desperate to have her missing twin brother give her away at our wedding."

The woman sighed as she turned back to face him. "That is so sweet." She hesitated, but only a moment longer. "There was this young woman that Judy had befriended when she worked at that old folks' home down in Missoula. Her name was Sheila. I saw her a few times when she came up to visit." Luella shook her head, lips pursed in disapproval. "I didn't like the look of her, but Judy was a sucker for anyone less off than she was. Sheila had had a hard life apparently and looked up to Judy."

He could see where that would have pleased Judy, who'd had a tough life herself. "Are you telling me Judy gave this young woman the baby?"

"I fear she did," Luella said, her voice cracking. "Broke my heart. That sweet innocent baby boy turned over to someone too immature, too irresponsible, too incapable of even taking care of herself let alone another life."

"How can I find Sheila?" he asked, hoping Luella had more than just the woman's first name to give him.

"I never knew her last name." His heart fell. "But I did hear from Judy that Sheila had gotten married. Said Sheila'd had a baby. Married some man named Grandville."

Buck knew the name. It was an old money Montana name. "You think the baby Sheila allegedly gave birth to was the baby boy Judy had given her?" Luella nodded. "You remember which Grandville she married?"

"Darrow Grandville," Luella said, not hiding her distaste for the man.

"I don't think I've ever heard of Darrow Grandville," Buck said, surprised.

"He was a cousin of the Grandvilles of Butte. Thought he was something, him and his fancy car, but I wasn't fooled." She shook her head. "I knew nothing good could come of it. Not a year later, Sheila was back—without the baby or the husband. Judy said Darrow had gotten into some kind of trouble and had to go underground, so to speak. I didn't ask about the baby. I didn't want to know."

"Underground?" he repeated.

Luella waved a hand through the air. "Some place outside of Butte, not really a ranch. The way Judy described it, the place was a hideout for outlaws. She always exaggerated, though. The ranch had a jewel in the name." She narrowed her eyes for a moment as if straining to come up with it. "Emerald Acres or something like that. I'm sorry. It's been too long."

"That will help," Buck said, hoping it was true.

"You think you can find him?" she asked, sounding as skeptical as he felt. "I mean for all we know, he didn't survive."

"I have to find him. Or at least find out what happened to him. If he's alive, his twin sister needs him at her wedding. As the groom, I'll turn over every rock looking for him."

As he left, he called the Colt Brothers Investigation office. "I need to find a ranch that existed near Butte almost thirty years ago. Might have been called Emerald Acres or something with a gemstone name."

"I'll put Tommy on it," James Colt assured him. "Anything else?"

"I'm also looking for a man named Darrow Grandville."

"Grandville? Like the Grandvilles of Butte?"

"A cousin apparently, a disreputable one possibly. He might have had my future bride's twin with him when he got into trouble and had to go to the ranch hideout."

"Great," James said. "I'd be careful with the Grandvilles."

Buck laughed. "Last I heard, they'd gone legit."

"Yeah. Crooks in high places are still crooks and even more dangerous. Also it's Butte. Tough town if you cross the wrong people."

"So I've heard."

"Let me guess," James said. "You're headed for Butte."

"Tell Tommy to call me if he finds anything on the ranch or Darrow. I might have to rattle some cages."

"I'll pay your bail," James said, and hung up.

DJ MENTALLY KICKED HIMSELF, wishing he hadn't told Sadie so much about his life with his uncle. He blamed it on being back in Butte. Memories assailed him the moment he started up the mountain to the old part of town. His uncle had loved Butte. He'd made a lot of money here and had been almost killed doing it several times. His uncle always said that he wouldn't have survived if it wasn't for DJ.

The two of them hadn't just been on the run from hotel managers and the dozens of people his uncle conned. "If anyone asks you why you aren't in school, you need to have a lie ready," Charley had warned. "Otherwise, they'll take you away from me, put you in a foster home, force you to go to school. Believe me, that's the last thing you want to happen."

Charley had grown up being kicked from home to home before he'd taken off on his own at sixteen and learned the grift from old codgers he met on the street. He taught everything he knew about the con to DJ. Everything else, DJ had learned when he was young from reading and television. Most hotels had books lying around that people had left behind. If desperate, there was usually a Gideon Bible in a motel room.

Once he was older, DJ got his GED and applied for college. Four years later he had a business degree and a legit job that he held on to for almost seven years. Poker night was just a way to pick up some spare change. Then he heard that his uncle Charley needed his help. He quit the job that he later admitted he hated, but before he could reach his uncle, Charley was arrested and sent to prison. That's when he met Sadie's godfather and went to work paying off his uncle's debt and buying him protection while inside. Charley died in prison two years ago of a heart attack.

DJ seldom looked back. That was something else his uncle had taught him. "Spend time looking behind you and you'll trip over your own two feet," Charley used to say. But being here brought so much of it back, the good, the bad and the downright ugly, he thought.

He tried to concentrate on setting up the poker

game rather than going down a very bumpy memory lane. He'd picked up his phone to call Sadie a dozen times, needing to hear her voice, needing to know that he wasn't making a mistake, but he hadn't called.

He knew she was busy playing her part. She was a pro. Meanwhile, he'd been playing poker in penny-ante games around town, looking for a front for the game. He finally found Bob Martin, a small-time poker player with friends with deep enough pockets. It just couldn't be obvious that DJ was behind the game or that he needed players who had money to lose.

DJ told Bob that he knew of a woman with money to burn who liked to play poker but wasn't very good, and the game was set for Friday night. Bob said he even had the perfect place, a local poker spot in the back room of a Chinese restaurant in the older part of town. DJ called Titus with the time and place.

Then he called Sadie.

BUCK WAS ON the outskirts of Butte when he got the call. Up here, the snow was deeper, the day darker, as the sun would soon be disappearing behind the mountains that closed in the city.

"It was the Diamond Deluxe Ranch," Tommy Colt said. "It was owned by a man named Charley Diamond. Word is, it was an enclave for outlaws. Diamond lost it about fifteen years ago to back taxes."

"Charley Diamond? Why does that name sound familiar?" Buck asked. Tommy had no idea. "Think

I'll see if Willie might recognize it. Anything on Darrow Grandville?"

"Dead. Killed in a bar fight twenty-four years ago."

Buck took the news like a blow. Ansley's twin would have been five years old. What had happened to him? "Tell me how to find the ranch."

"It's now part of a larger working ranch, so the place is probably not occupied." He gave him directions.

"Thanks." He disconnected and called Sheriff Willie Colt. "Charley Diamond," he said without preamble when Willie answered. "Ring a bell?"

"Charley Diamond? Nope, but if it's important I could ask around."

"If you wouldn't mind. He used to own a ranch up here outside of Butte. A place for outlaws to hide out apparently. Darrow Grandville might have been one of them. Grandville hooked up with a friend of Judy Ramsey's named Sheila. That's all I have on her. But she might have gotten Ansley's twin. Problem is, a year later, after hooking up with Grandville, she didn't have the kid anymore."

"I'll see what I can find out. Where are you?"

"On my way to visit the Grandvilles."

"Really bad idea from what I've heard about the family," Willie said, and disconnected.

Buck wasn't surprised that he had to push his way in to see Titus Grandville in his penthouse-floor office.

"I'm sorry, but if you don't have an appointment—"

He walked past the receptionist down the hallway. The views through the windows he passed were of historic Butte with its old mining rigs as well as decaying remnants of elaborate brickwork buildings from a time when it had been the largest city west of Chicago.

Titus Grandville was on his feet by the time Buck walked into his office. "I've already called security."

"I just need to ask you a couple of quick questions." He held out his hand as he approached the man. "Buck Crawford. I'm with Colt Brothers Investigation in Lonesome."

Titus raised a brow, but made no move to shake hands. "Private dick?"

Buck dropped his hand. "I prefer PI. I need to ask you about Darrow Grandville."

"I don't know anyone by that name. Had you called, I could have saved you the trip. Now if that's all."

"Darrow is your cousin. He was arrested in Butte about twenty-odd years ago and might have been staying out on the Diamond Deluxe."

"Before my time," Titus said.

"He might have had a woman with him. Sheila? And a little boy somewhere around one or two at the time."

Grandville was shaking his head. "I told you—"

"You don't remember, right. Well, I'm looking for the boy. He would be twenty-nine now."

"Why are you looking for him anyway?"

"Client confidentiality."

Titus smirked as he settled into his massive office chair. "He wanted for something?"

"A wedding. He needs to give the bride away."

Grandville laughed. "Quite the dangerous case you're on, PI."

"Maybe your father would remember," Buck said as he turned to leave. "I've got time. I'll drop by his place. Maybe his memory is better than yours. Shouldn't be hard to find him since your childhood home is on the historic register."

"Don't bother my father. He isn't well."

Buck was headed for the door.

Grandville was on his feet now. "I'm serious. Leave my father out of this. He doesn't know anyone named Darrow. Or Sheila or anything about a kid."

"I guess I'll see." He walked out with Grandville cursing after him.

SADIE HAD BEEN getting into her new role by spending money. She'd ordered room service and then gone shopping. She'd bought her godfather a Western bolo tie as a gift. She'd picked up a pair of red cowboy boots for herself along with some boot-cut jeans and a large leather purse with a horse carved into it. The purse was plenty big enough for everything she needed.

After she'd returned from an outing, the hotel clerk had called to say that she had a package down at the main desk. Inside it, she'd found a handgun like the one she usually used and ammunition. She'd cleaned and loaded it, telling herself that the next time she saw DJ would be no different than any other night she'd worked with him. Except she was playing a different role and her godfather wouldn't have set up the place and the players.

While it had been dangerous the other times, she'd felt as if things had been under control. She feared that wouldn't be the case this time as she loaded the gun and put it in her new shoulder bag. DJ was too personally involved this time, and that worried her.

After DJ's call, she now had the time and place. All she had to do was wait. She'd already planned what she would wear, who she would be. She and DJ had signals so they could communicate if needed. Usually, it wasn't needed because they both knew the other person so well.

Just the thought that this would be their last game together made her sad. She knew she was being silly. When her godfather had come to her about working with DJ, she'd thought he'd lost his mind.

"This guy is one hell of a poker player," he'd said. "With you as his wingman, the two of you can't lose."

She'd been skeptical at best, especially after she'd met him. DJ was too handsome, too cocky, too much a cowboy even without the Stetson. He seemed like a wild card—the kind of man who could get her killed.

But after one game, she'd been a believer. He was as good as her godfather had said. And under all that cocky cowboy arrogance there was something special.

Isn't that why DJ had gotten to her? Why she knew she'd risk her life for this cowboy without a moment's hesitation?

Was that what she was about to do?

Chapter Seven

Buck figured Titus Grandville would have called for security at his father's mansion. He decided to let security cool their heels for a few hours while he drove out to the old Diamond Deluxe Ranch first.

He drove south, down the mountain from historic Butte to a strip of newer businesses. Like a lot of towns in Montana, the old mining city had seen better days. Buck quickly found himself in the mountains.

Tommy had been right. There wasn't much left of the Diamond Deluxe Ranch and yet he could read the name branded into the weathered wood arch over the road in. A few outbuildings stood along the edge of the road. Through the pines he saw a dilapidated two-story farmhouse, the paint long peeled off, the porch rotted, little glass left in the windows. There was a chicken coop and what could have once been a bunkhouse.

Buck told himself there was nothing here to find, yet he knew he couldn't leave until he looked around.

He had to climb up through a deep snowdrift that had blown in across the front porch. The front door was ajar, snow drifted across the weathered hardwood floor inside. He tested the floor. It creaked and groaned but didn't give way as he entered.

A stairway led up to the second floor. He could hear something moving around up there. Pack rats? He started up the stairs, more sounds of movement as small animals scrambled for cover. He found a few old mattresses, a pile of metal bed rails and a couple of broken-down dressers.

There was nothing here of DelRae's twin. For all Buck knew DJ had never even been here. The baby Sheila and Darrow Grandville had with them might not even be the missing twin. He coughed, aware of the dust and other scents in the air, none of them making him want to spend another minute here.

As he started for the top of the stairs, he saw something that made him stop. He recognized the painstakingly carved marks down one side of the door's wood frame. He still had those on the inside of his bedroom. It was a growth chart. Buck stepped closer and felt his heart bump in his chest. He crouched to read the crudely carved dates in the pine. A child had stood here to be measured. He leaned closer, running his finger over what appeared to be initials. DJ.

Buck broke into a grin. Ansley's missing twin had been here. His growth proved that he'd survived to live here at least until... He quickly did the math.

His middle teens. That's when the dates on the marks stopped.

Frowning, he noticed that it wasn't just DJ's growth chart carved into this piece of old pine. He tried to make out the name. Keira? A younger child from the dates. He took several photos, anxious to call his bride-to-be. He hadn't found her twin, but at least he knew that DJ had survived to his teens in this place.

Buck did the math, comparing the last date on the chart to when Tommy had told him that Charley Diamond had lost the ranch. What had happened to these kids? DJ had been in his middle to late teens, but whoever Keira was, that child had been much younger. Where would they have gone? Social services?

He called Tommy, then he headed for Old Man Grandville's. He told himself that he'd call Ansley later with the news, hoping he would know more by then.

The Grandville home had been a mansion in its day. Built in the late 1800s during the city's opulent past on what was known as the richest hill on earth, it was the home of one of the city's high society. Three stories with gingerbread brickwork, ornate wood filigree and leaded glass windows, it had stood the test of time.

Buck parked on the steep street. No sign of security. He climbed out and walked through the wrought iron gate, up the sidewalk and onto the wide front porch. At the massive wood door, he rang the bell.

To his surprise, an elderly man in apparently fine health answered the door. He was dressed in slacks and sweater, loafers on his feet. He wasn't tall or handsome, but there was an air about him of arrogant dominance. He could see where the son, Titus, had gotten it from.

"Marcus Grandville," Buck said. "I'm Buck Crawford, a private investigator with—"

"I know who you are," the man said. "You're here about Darrow. Titus called and warned me you might be stopping by. I have a few minutes before I need to leave." He waved him into what had once been the parlor. Now it felt more like a den. "This shouldn't take long, but if you'd like to sit…"

He took one of the chairs facing the elderly Grandville.

"Darrow," Marcus said. "What about him?"

"He's your nephew?"

The older man gave a nod. "*Was* my nephew. Why are you asking about him after all these years?"

"He married a woman named Sheila about thirty years ago and they moved up this way. I'm trying to find Sheila."

"I have no idea where she is after all this time."

"But you met her."

"I suppose I must have."

Buck tried not to grit his teeth. "Did she have a child with her?"

Marcus frowned. He could tell that the man was about to say no when Marcus surprised him. "A boy with dark hair and pale blue eyes. One look at him and I knew he was no Grandville. Any fool could tell that. Any fool except my nephew."

"He thought the boy was his?"

"Darrow took after the other side of our family," Marcus said in answer.

"Sheila returned to Lonesome without the boy after they split," Buck said. "What did Darrow do with the boy?"

The man shrugged. "Had him with him the last time I saw my nephew. He was hanging around some ranch outside of town."

"The Diamond Deluxe?"

Marcus's eyes lit up for a moment. "Charley Diamond's place, that's right. Haven't thought about that place in years. Look, I have an appointment." He started to get to his feet, but Buck stopped him.

"I know the young man I'm looking for lived out at that ranch," he said. "I suspect your nephew left him out there. What I need to know is what happened to the boy after that."

The elderly man sighed. "Charley lost that place, you know." Buck nodded. "I think I might know who you're looking for. After Charley lost the ranch, he and a teenage boy were running cons around the state. You think DJ Diamond was the kid Darrow thought was his? Mind if I ask why you're interested in Diamond?"

"It's a long story, but he has family looking for him."

"Family?" Marcus huffed, looking skeptical, as he rose, interview over.

"One more question," Buck said as he rose as well. "Have you ever heard of someone named Keira?"

He saw the answer in the man's face an instant before Marcus caught himself. "I really have to go. Sorry I couldn't have been more help."

"On the contrary, you have been very helpful. I can show myself out."

"TITUS," MARCUS SAID the moment his oldest son answered the phone. "That PI from Lonesome was just here."

Titus swore. "Where were Rafe and Butch? They were supposed to make sure he didn't bother you."

"I sent them away," Marcus said with a curse. "I'm quite capable of taking care of myself and I was curious why he would be asking about Darrow and that woman, Sheila. Darrow's dead and who knows what happened to Sheila. Did the PI ask you about Keira?"

A worrisome silence, then, "No, why would he ask about her?"

"That's what I want to know. Didn't I hear that she owes us money?"

"I'd really like to know how you hear these things, Dad."

Marcus waved that off. "Why would the PI be asking about her?"

"I have no idea. Her husband, Luca, is the one who owes the money, but we've been putting pressure on her. But we're going to get it settled by the end of the week. She got her buddy from the ranch to come help her out."

"What buddy from the ranch?" Marcus asked, afraid he already knew the answer.

"DJ Diamond."

Marcus swore. "That's who the PI was looking for. Why didn't you tell me that DJ Diamond was in town?"

"I had no idea you'd care. He paid me a visit, threatened to throw me out the window. But he'll pay off Keira's debt. Calls her his sister."

He didn't like this. As much as he loved his son, Titus often made poor decisions. Soon he would be in charge of their family fortune. The thought terrified him. "How much does Luca owe us?"

"Seventy-five. Diamond's a conman. Offered to settle for half the price. He's an arrogant fool like his uncle."

"DJ was Charley Diamond's protégé," Marcus said. "I wouldn't underestimate him if I were you. The last thing you want him to do is move in on our territory. Settle this and let me know when he leaves town."

"I can handle him. I have a plan."

"That's what worries me," Marcus said.

JAMES ANSWERED THE phone when Buck called the office. "I'm staying in Butte." Since going out to the Diamond Deluxe and talking to the Grandvilles, Buck was more convinced that DJ Diamond was the missing twin.

"Find something?" James asked.

"A few pieces of the puzzle seem to be coming

together," he said. "It looks like the baby that Sheila and Darrow Grandville had was called DJ. That's assuming that Sheila did name the boy Del Junior or at least call him DJ." He told James about what he'd found out at the ranch inside the farmhouse owned by Charley Diamond, then about his visit to Titus Grandville.

"Titus Grandville." James said the name like a curse. "Anyone from this part of Montana has nothing good to say about that man."

"He pretended he'd never heard of Charley Diamond or the ranch," Buck said.

"These guys all know each other. Might not have traveled in the same circles but they're all connected."

"After Grandville lied to me, I went to see his old man."

"He's still alive?"

"Titus told me he wasn't well. Another lie from what I could tell. Marcus was more up-front, confirming what I'd already found out. Said he did remember the boy being with his nephew. Also said he remembered the Diamond Deluxe Ranch and DJ running cons with his uncle when he was a teen. I got the impression that Marcus doesn't know what Titus is up to, though, but I could be wrong. He definitely didn't want me talking to his father."

"Titus always was the worst of the bunch," James said. "And that was saying a lot."

"Marcus told me that after Charley Diamond lost the ranch, he and DJ traveled around Montana running cons." He didn't have to say that he was worried about the kind of man he was going to find.

"Buck, are you sure about this? Maybe finding him isn't the best idea."

"I can't stop now. I haven't told Ansley any of this. I'm thinking that I should wait until I find him."

"I think that's wise."

"I'm going to hang around and see what Titus is up to. I just have a feeling about him. I've rattled enough cages that I suspect he'll lead me to DJ if he knows where he is."

"Watch your back," James said. "You're in the Grandvilles' sandbox and we already know that they don't play nice."

SADIE TOLD HERSELF that she was ready. In the days since she'd arrived here, she hadn't seen DJ. She'd missed him. Knowing that this might be their last poker game together had her feeling melancholy. She'd known from the beginning that one day it would end. DJ would have paid off his uncle's debt. They would have no reason to see each other.

Her future felt hollow. She really hadn't realized how much she was going to miss that arrogant grin of his. Or the way she often found him looking at her. Every time, she saw that gleam in his eyes, it warmed her clear to her toes. She kept telling herself that she'd never fall for his charm. She didn't want to be one of his women. But now she could admit that the thought of never seeing him again made her ache with longing.

She was looking forward to tonight's game just to see him. Although she was nervous. She felt as if too much was riding on tonight. She'd taken an Uber part of the ride down the mountain and walked the rest of the way through the falling snow to get a feel for where she was. It appeared to be an even older part of the city, the area more industrial than residential or commercial. Even under a heavy blanket of the pristine new snow still falling, it looked as if this place hadn't seen better days in a very long time.

She didn't need to question why DJ might have agreed to this site. It was the kind of neighborhood where no one would hear a gunshot. But that was a double-edged sword when dealing with people you didn't know or trust.

As she stepped down the alley, she saw the door he'd described and the sign over it. It appeared to be the back entrance to a Chinese food restaurant—if still operational. She didn't see anyone else around, but knew she had the right place. DJ had been explicit in his directions.

The metal door was heavy as she pulled it open and looked down a long, dimly lit hallway. Time to get into character, she thought as she stepped in and let the door close loudly behind her. Swearing just loud enough to let the men know she was coming, she brushed snow from her coat and yelled, "Could you have found a darker place?"

The hall was long with several closed doors. She kept going, following the acrid scent of cheap cigars and the murmur of voices. At the end of the hall, she

turned to the right toward another hallway. One of
the doors was open a few yards farther. She could
hear the men's voices more clearly along with the
scrape of chair legs on a wood floor and the rattle
of ice being dropped into a glass.

She stepped into the open doorway and, leaning
against the jamb, she took in the men already starting to gather around the table.

"Why am I craving pot stickers?" she demanded,
and laughed as they all turned toward her. As she
entered the room, she removed her coat, sweeping in
as if the place wasn't a dump. She'd worn designer
jeans and a lightweight sweater that accentuated her
curves but modestly. She wore a scarf loosely tied
around her neck and diamond earrings that glittered
every time she tucked a lock of her long blond hair
back behind an ear. Her coat was a classic expensive
wool. Nothing too flashy.

"Anyone save me a spot at the table?" she asked.

One of the men jumped up to pull out an empty
chair for her. She wouldn't be sitting directly across
from DJ, but she wouldn't be sitting next to him,
either. "This should work," she said, and looked at
each of the players as she sat down. "Good evening,
gentlemen." She held her large leather bag in her lap.

"Buy-in is ten thousand dollars," said a florid-
faced, heavyset man with the offending cigar in
one hand and a drink in the other. He motioned to
a makeshift bar set up over by a sad-looking couch.
She saw a tray of mismatched glasses, a bucket of
ice, several bottles of booze, a container with a dol-

lar sign on the side, and a cooler on the floor with beer iced down. "Booze? Put your money in the kitty. I'm Bob. We're using cash, no chips. We're the Old West here. I'll need to see your money."

"I'm Whitney," she said as she met the man's gaze through the smoke, smiled and reached into her bag to pull out an envelope full of cash. She gave a tilt of her head. "Ten thousand. I'm betting you want to count it." She slid it over to him.

He thumbed through the hundreds, then passed it back with a lopsided grin.

Sadie took a thousand dollars from the envelope and laid it on the table in front of her. She wondered which players DJ had gotten into the game other than her and Bob. One of the men at this table was the real mark. Bob was the kind to have invited at least one of his buddies as well. The trick was figuring out who was who.

She'd never been more aware of DJ. Having him so close was like a separate pulse beating under her skin. She felt the heat of him and wanted more than anything to see that arrogant grin of his, to feel his eyes on her, to connect with the man who'd gambled his way into her thoughts and her heart.

Bob introduced everyone only by first name starting with the man to his right as he went around the table. Max, the large truck driver in the Kenworth jacket and T-shirt that read I Drop Big Loads. Her, then Lloyd in the canvas jacket and fishing shirt. Next to him was Keith, the youngest in a hoody, jeans and untied trainers. Then Frank, the oldest of the bunch with short gray hair and the air of an ex-military man or retired cop. He gave her a nod. She watched him line up his bills perfectly in front of him. And last but not least, DJ, sitting next to Bob.

Sadie tried to still the unease she felt as she looked around the table. It was an odd gathering. She noticed that only two of them were drinking, Bob and Lloyd, the fisherman. She had no idea who was the true mark. As she started to hook her purse over the back of the chair, it slipped and fell to the floor.

Lloyd started to reach down to pick it up.

"I have it," she said, and grabbed it before he could. He moved his chair over a little to make room.

"Sorry," he said, avoiding her gaze.

"Let's play some poker," Frank said impatiently. "I don't have all night."

"I agree with Frank. Let's play." Sadie bent down to retrieve her purse. As she did, she glanced under the table and saw Frank shift in his chair, his slacks riding up to expose the gun in his ankle holster—and froze.

Chapter Eight

Sadie tried to stay calm, but her heart was pounding as she straightened. She could feel DJ's gaze on her and wasn't surprised when he spoke.

"Excuse me," he said. "Does anyone else have a new deck of cards? No offense, Bob." He looked around the table, his gaze lingering on her for just a few seconds longer than the others.

She pulled her purse up on her lap, reached inside, but instead of pulling out a deck of the marked cards, she took out her lipstick and applied a fresh coat before putting it away. Out of the corner of her eye she saw Bob roll his eyes. Frank said something rude under his breath.

But it was DJ's reaction to her "abort" signal that she was most interested in. He stared at her for a moment before shaking his head ever so slightly. He wasn't going to walk away.

"We're going old-school tonight," Bob said, opening one of the packs of cards he'd brought. "Five-card stud, jacks or better to open, minimum bid ten bucks,

no pot limit." Bob grinned. "That ain't too rich for
your blood, is it, cowboy?" he said to DJ. He began
shuffling with practiced expertise. After a few more
elaborate shuffles, he set down the deck and Trucker
Max cut them.

Sadie could feel DJ's gaze on her and shook her
head imperceptibly. She didn't have to look at him
to feel his disapproval. She knew what was riding on
this for him—and his sister. But she had also learned
to follow her instincts. She'd felt uncomfortable the
moment she'd walked into this room. After seeing
that one of their opponents was armed—and possibly ex-military or a retired cop—there was no way
she was going through with the original plan.

Unfortunately, DJ was ignoring her advice and
now she had no idea what he was planning—except
they wouldn't be using the marked deck of cards in
her bag—and she hoped not the gun resting there,
either.

So where did that leave them?

DJ HAD LIVED his life calculating the risk—and then
playing the odds. But he'd never regretted it more
than he did right now. He looked over at Sadie. He'd
missed her. All the time he'd been putting things
together, his thoughts had kept straying to her. He
knew she was doing what he'd asked of her. That
was Sadie. He could count on her. He just hoped she
could count on him. She hadn't hesitated about coming to Montana to help him. He'd known she would

fly up here to do whatever he needed done. He'd needed her, and of course she'd come.

What he couldn't understand was why. She didn't owe him anything. Half the time, he thought she didn't like him. It wasn't the first time he'd heard her call him an arrogant fool. He figured she'd be relieved now that they wouldn't be working together for her godfather. She was free.

He'd often wondered if there was a man in her life. He'd been glad that she'd never mentioned one—let alone let him see her with anyone. DJ knew he'd never think any man was good enough for her. Not that she would ask his opinion.

Now he tried to read her face. The woman had the best poker face he'd ever seen. She gave nothing away. But he knew that she'd been worried. He'd seen her concern. She'd heard it in his voice. She'd known this was personal. They all knew that when it got personal, it got more dangerous. He wasn't just taking a chance with his own life; he was jeopardizing hers. He had no idea why she'd wanted to abort. He'd known her long enough that he knew she wouldn't have done that unless she'd seen something she thought he hadn't.

His gaze locked with hers, but only for a moment before she looked away. She thought he was making a mistake. He could tell that she was angry with him. It wouldn't be the first time. She'd called him an arrogant fool, an arrogant cowboy and probably worse. But tonight was the first time she'd refused to use the marked cards.

He trusted her instincts. She'd seen or felt something that had made her change her mind. She wanted him to walk away. Had she sensed that one of the players was a wild card? Or had she seen something that scared her? Not that it mattered. He couldn't quit now.

Sorry, Sadie, no can do. He wanted to tell her to trust him. But he feared her trust might be misplaced tonight. Charley had taught him the con, always warning him to step away from the table if he didn't think he could win. Poker was a game of skill, one DJ had perfected. But most everything else was a crapshoot. You read the situation as best you could, but ultimately, you had no control over what other people did—or didn't do. All you had were your gut instincts and years of learning to read people.

DJ hoped to hell that he knew what he was doing tonight. He'd gotten Sadie into this. He signaled for her to walk away after a few hands. Leave not feeling well. Make up a lie. Just leave.

But when he met her eyes, he saw not just anger but stubborn determination. Damn the woman, she would see this through. It was up to him now. Play out the hand he'd been dealt or throw in his cards and walk. He didn't have to look at Sadie. They both knew he wouldn't walk away.

SADIE CONCENTRATED ON the game and her opponents rather than DJ. She drew three cards on the first hand, picked up a couple of fours to go with the one she had, bet big and lost. The others noticed that she'd bet on a losing hand. She would play her part. But she would also be watching the table.

Frank had folded early in the betting, while Keith, slouching in his chair, was throwing good money after bad. Bob took the pot and passed the deal to trucker Max, and the game continued.

Sadie won and lost. So did DJ, although his pile of money kept growing. Keith, the kid, lost, got angry and stormed away from the table to crash on an old couch in the corner after Bob refused to spot him credit.

And then there were six of them and suddenly, the game turned serious. The pots got bigger, the smoke thicker, the smell of sweat stronger. Sadie felt the tension rise. She knew DJ felt it, too, but he looked calm, almost too calm.

Earlier, he had signaled for her to leave. *Cash out. Walk away.* She couldn't. She had tried to warn him. He hadn't listened. Her options were limited. Keep playing or quit and walk away from not only the game, but also DJ, and not look back. If she walked, that would be the end of them. He would never trust her again—even with him being the one to tell her to leave. Their time together was ending as it was. She couldn't bear the thought that she'd let him down when he needed her most.

No, she thought, there was no way she was leaving him here alone. There was nothing more she could do but stay in the game and see this to the end. She thought about the gun in her purse and hoped she wouldn't have to use it. The load wasn't enough to do much harm to DJ if he had worn his vest under his shirt and jean jacket. But it would stop someone. Problem was that she didn't want to use it any more than she had the marked cards.

All she could hope was that her instincts were wrong, that Frank wasn't the wild card she feared he was, and that DJ's stubborn determination would carry them through as the cards moved around the table. Bob opened a new deck after a short break, and they continued.

Bob was losing and getting drunker. His dealing was sloppy. Sadie watched him. If she hadn't been able to smell the booze wafting off him, she might have been worried that it was all an act, and he was dealing off the bottom of the deck. He lost the next pot and handed off the cards to Max.

The trucker had been playing well. He and DJ had about the same amount of money in front of them. Lloyd the fisherman had played a conservative game, folding early, and yet staying in the game. The armed Frank was good at the game. Maybe too good. He gave nothing away, including his money.

Her turn was coming up again to deal. She'd lost just enough so that the others didn't take her seriously. As it got later, she found herself getting more nervous. The trucker began losing badly, hemorrhaging money. He wasn't smart enough to stop. She could see him getting more anxious.

Bob had begun to sweat as his pile of bills dwindled. He'd been making bad bets on even worse hands. He kept rubbing the back of his neck, shifting in his chair, getting up to make himself another drink he didn't need. He knew he was going down and this had been his show. The pressure was clearly getting to him.

"Come on, we don't have all night," Bob kept complaining. The trucker, too, was restless. Only Frank seemed unperturbed when the game slowed. All of it put her on alert.

DJ must have noticed that things were coming to a head. On the next hand, he raised the bet. The others either thought he was bluffing or just didn't want to fold in defeat, so they stayed in, no doubt convinced that they had the better hand.

They'd come to the end of the night, one way or another. Even Frank was in deep with this hand. Bob would be broke if he didn't win the pot, and Lloyd was down badly. The game was about over.

Sadie stayed in with three queens. "I'll call your bluff," she said, and met DJ's gaze with a look that said, "I hope you know what you're doing."

He grinned as she tossed her money onto the growing pile. He was going to have to show his hand.

BUCK HAD BEEN parked down the street from the Grandville building for hours and was beginning to wonder if he'd missed Titus, when the man came out the back door and headed for a large SUV parked across the alley. He seemed in a hurry as he slid behind the wheel.

From down the block, Buck was glad that his instincts had been right. Now he feared that he'd wasted his time. Maybe Grandville would only go home for the night. But it didn't take long to realize that Titus wasn't headed home.

Instead, the man drove down the mountain to an older, more decrepit part of Butte. The streets became darker, the commercial buildings got more derelict looking before the banker pulled over, parked and after getting out, walked down the street to where he ducked into an alley.

Buck stopped down the block in front of an old gas station with a condemned sign out front. He checked his gun, put on his side holster and turned off his cell phone before tucking it into his coat pocket and getting out. It had been snowing off and on all day. Falling snow spun around him as he walked toward where he'd seen Grandville disappear. By the time he turned down the alley, huge lacy snowflakes were fluttering down, making it hard to see more than a few yards ahead.

His gut told him he was onto something even as his head said this might be a complete waste of his time. This nighttime adventure might not lead him any closer to DJ Diamond because it might be nothing more than a booty call. Titus might have a woman he was secretly meeting. Not that this appeared to be a residential area.

At the top of the alley, he could see footprints in the snow. The new flakes hadn't covered them yet. They led to a back entrance of what appeared to be a Chinese food restaurant. The sign was faded. He wondered if the place was even still in business. He moved down the alley through the falling snow, his footfalls cushioned by the new snow.

At the door, Buck grabbed the handle and pulled, half expecting it to be locked. It wasn't. He stood to the side for a few moments listening before he peered in, then stepped through into the semidarkness, closing the door quietly behind him. He stood stone still for a moment to let his eyes adjust to the lack of light.

There appeared to be a solitary bulb at the far end of the hallway. He headed for it, following the murmur of voices.

SADIE HAD BEEN watching DJ closely. He hadn't cheated. But she could feel the tension in the room spark and sizzle. The pot was huge and DJ had already won a lot of money. Earlier he'd been playing with a stack of hundreds. A few minutes later, the stack had shrunk but not so noticeably that the others had seen him pocket the bills. He didn't want anyone to see how far ahead he was. He was playing smart, but she feared that wouldn't matter. Frank's being armed had her nerves frayed. Maybe he always came to games armed. Or not.

Sadie realized that she was holding her breath and told herself to breathe. She had to be ready if things went south. *When* things went south, she amended. The thing about carrying a gun was knowing when to pull it. The rule of thumb had always been: never pull a weapon unless you were going to use it—and quickly—before someone took it away and used it on you.

Her purse was hooked on the back of her chair, easily accessible—but not quickly. She had her gaze on DJ, but her true focus was on Frank, whom she was watching closely from the corner of her eye. If he reached down for the gun strapped on his ankle, she was going to have to pull hers. She would have only seconds to act.

For all she knew Frank wasn't a retired cop, but still an active-duty older cop. Even her godfather would have advised against shooting a cop—especially one with a loaded gun at a poker game. Ex-military or cop or just cop-looking older man with a gun, Frank was the wild card.

It had crossed her mind that Frank's true purpose here tonight might not be to play poker at all. She'd gotten the impression that DJ had enemies here in Butte. Her godfather had told her that teenage DJ had worked cons for years with his uncle until he went out on his own. She had no idea what kind of trouble DJ's sister was in, other than financially, or with whom. But if someone wanted to draw DJ out to even an old score, they now had him back in Montana on their home turf.

Sadie knew it was her fear making her think these

things. But hadn't she, from the start, been worried that his concern for Keira had overridden his survival instincts?

She met his gaze across the table in those seconds as the last player threw his money into the pot and called to see DJ's hand. Her heart ached at the look in his eyes. He had known that this might be all about him. She held his incredibly blue eyes. *Tell me what you want me to do.* He gave a slight shake of his head. Nothing? He didn't want her to do *anything*? But it was what else she saw there that gutted her. *I'm sorry.*

No, she wanted to scream. DJ had to know her better than that. She wouldn't let Frank kill him in cold blood—not if she could prevent it. She could have heard a tear drop in the tense silence as DJ started to let his cards fall on the table.

Chapter Nine

Buck reached the end of the hallway and saw a short hallway off to his right. One of the doors was partially open. The smell of cigar smoke wafted out. Quietly, he moved closer until he could look inside.

From what he could see through the haze of smoke, there was a poker game going on. He didn't see Titus, but he knew he was here somewhere. Even from the doorway, he could feel the tension in the room as thick as the cigar smoke.

There were five men and one woman at the table, another man on a couch in the corner. Past the woman he could see a pile of money in the middle of the table. High-stakes game, it appeared. He could smell the sweat and the booze. His anxiety rose. Where was Titus? Why had he driven down here tonight? The whole scene had Buck on edge. He'd seen gunplay break out over a game with a lot less at stake.

He heard the heavy man with the cigar say, "All right, DJ. Let's see what you've got." There was an edge to his voice.

Everyone seemed to be waiting on the cowboy who was about Buck's age. He had dark hair and even from here, Buck could see that he had pale blue eyes. DJ Diamond?

The room fell silent as if everyone in it was holding their breath. DJ shoved back his cowboy hat and grinned as he let the cards drop faceup on the table.

EVEN BEFORE DJ's cards hit the table, the room seemed to explode in a roar of voices and movement. Everyone was moving at once. Sadie had gotten only a glimpse of DJ's cards. He had a royal flush? No wonder everyone was yelling. She would have sworn that he hadn't cheated, but then again, DJ was a man of many talents.

She wanted to look at him, to see the truth in his eyes, but her gaze was on Frank. His chair scraped as he threw down his cards, one fluttering to the floor, and shoved back from the table.

Sadie reached into her purse, avoiding looking at DJ. If Frank came up with his gun, she'd be ready. Her hand dived into her purse, closing around the pistol's grip. She could feel movement all around her as players threw down their cards and rose, but her gaze stayed on Frank as he reached down. She gripped the gun tighter. She was about to bring it up when he straightened, coming up —not with a gun, but with the card he'd dropped.

As he threw the card on the table, his gaze locked with hers. But only for a second. Just long enough to tell her that she'd made a huge mistake. It wasn't Frank that she and DJ had to worry about.

DJ ALWAYS EXPECTED TROUBLE. So he wasn't surprised when cards went flying, chairs crashed to the floor, drinks spilled as all but a couple of players were on their feet and yelling.

The tension had been rising like the heat around the table. Too much money had changed hands and tempers were flaring. It was the name of these kinds of supposedly friendly card games.

But this one had gone south much quicker than he'd expected. Bob was on his feet and so was Max, the trucker, and Frank, the older man he figured Sadie had tagged as a retired cop. He'd figured both Bob and the trucker for poor sports if they lost too much. But it was the younger man in the fishing shirt who surprised him.

He watched in horror as Lloyd reached over and grabbed Sadie's wrist. She had her hand in her purse. Now he watched as Lloyd twisted her wrist, making her cry out and the gun drop from her fingers back into the large bag.

As he unarmed her, he rose to step behind her. Before DJ could move, Lloyd locked his arm around her neck, drew a gun and pulled her to her feet. DJ rose slowly, putting his hands into the air as the barrel of the gun was pointed at his chest. All he could think was that Sadie had tried to warn him and he'd ignored her. He thought he knew what he was doing. Arrogant fool.

"Everyone just stay where you are," Lloyd ordered as he motioned with the weapon in his hands. "This is between me and Diamond."

Max and Bob quickly stepped away from the table and the huge pile of money in the middle. "Easy," DJ said. "It's just a friendly game of poker."

"Like hell," Lloyd said as Keith left the couch with a bag in his hand. "Cash us out," Lloyd told him. Keith grinned as he began to scoop the money into the bag, taking not just the pot, but any money that had been in front of the players.

"What's the deal here?" Bob asked, sounding confused and scared. It seemed pretty clear to DJ what was happening. He'd been set up and was now being ripped off along with everyone else.

"I don't want any trouble," the trucker said, stepping even farther back. Bob and Frank had both frozen where they stood at the sight of the gun in Lloyd's hand. Bob looked jittery, as if he badly needed a drink. Frank on the other hand stood watching expressionless, seeming to be assessing the situation.

DJ expected someone in the room to do something stupid before this was over. But he figured Lloyd was expecting the same thing. The man still had Sadie in a headlock and his own gun pointed in the general direction of the three of them; Bob was to his right, Frank to his far left. The trucker had moved closer to the door.

Unfortunately, the table was between DJ and Lloyd, not to mention the gun or the man's arm cutting off Sadie's air.

"Got a message for you, Diamond, from Mr. Grandville," Lloyd said. "Pay up and get out of town. You're not welcome in Butte."

The tension in the room kicked up a few more notches. Frank swore and stepped farther back. "What the hell?" Bob said angrily. "DJ, you didn't tell me you were mixed up with the Grandvilles." He looked like he wanted to take a swing at him.

DJ felt the tension reaching a fevered pitch. Why didn't Lloyd and Keith just take the money and leave if that's what this was about? Because they'd come for more than the money. He had to get Sadie away from them. She wasn't part of this. Unless they knew differently. In that case, they were both as good as dead.

"Which Grandville in particular sent this message?" he asked, surprised how calm he sounded. "Titus or Marcus?"

"Does it matter?" Lloyd snapped.

"Actually, it does."

"They both want you gone, along with that PI from Lonesome who's looking for you," Lloyd said. "Seems you have family looking for you. You must owe them money, too."

DJ frowned. He had a PI from Lonesome looking for him? Something about family? That didn't sound right. Actually, none of this felt right. According to Keira, her husband, Luca, was staying just outside of Lonesome in the mountains at Charley's cabin.

He met Sadie's gaze, his full of apology. She was fighting to breathe but still looked angry and determined. He tried not to show how afraid he was for her. All his instincts told him that this wasn't going to end well, and he had only himself to blame. But he knew that he would die trying to save her.

Sadie was filled with a cold dread as she watched the scene unfold. Lloyd kept cutting off her air. She'd leaned into him, trying to relieve some of the pressure as she calculated what they could do to get out of this. It wasn't her nature to give up. There was always a way out of a mess, wasn't there?

She'd hoped that Lloyd and Keith would just take the money and leave. But she could see that it wasn't going to happen. This was personal.

DJ had realized it, too. She saw it in those blue eyes of his. She couldn't bear seeing his regret. He thought he was about to get them both killed. She wasn't ready to give up so easily. Also she knew that he'd risk his life to save her. She couldn't live with his blood on her hands.

For a moment she was overwhelmed with her feelings for the cowboy. He'd gotten her into this, and she should have been furious with him. But instead, all she felt was love, and that alone made her angry with herself, with him and with this jackass who had her in a headlock.

The Grandvilles had apparently set them up, that much was clear. Lloyd had known about her and DJ. He'd known she had a gun. He'd also known that they were here to make money to pay back Titus Grandville.

When he'd grabbed her, twisting the gun from her hand and dropping it back into her shoulder bag as he pulled her to her feet, she'd been taken off guard. She'd been so sure that Frank was the one they had to fear.

Now as she watched the others, feeling the pressure rising to the point where everything was going to blow, she knew she couldn't wait much longer to do something. These men weren't through with her and DJ. She didn't think they would kill everyone in the room. But they weren't going to let her and DJ walk away. She would have to act.

For a moment, she'd been distracted by Bob, who definitely looked as if he wanted to pick a fight with DJ. So she hadn't seen how Frank had maneuvered himself out of her line of vision—and Lloyd's— behind DJ. Keith had gone back to the old sofa and was busy counting the money.

She thought that no one had noticed Frank as he reached down and came up with the gun except her. If he fired, she feared Lloyd would shoot DJ. But before she could squeeze in her next breath, the door into the room was suddenly flung open.

"Everyone. Drop your weapons!" yelled a cowboy with a gun standing in the doorway. "Hands up! No one gets hurt!"

All she could think in that instant was *This is it. This is the game that will get me killed—and DJ, too.*

Chapter Ten

Sadie had no idea who the man was. But the distraction was enough that she saw what might be her only chance—and so did DJ. He launched himself across the table toward her and Lloyd as she drove her elbow into Lloyd's ribs and grabbed for his gun. But not quickly enough. As DJ crashed into them, the gun went off, the sound of the shot deafening in the confines of the room.

Had DJ been hit? Her heart dropped.

The force of his attack sent all three of them to the floor, Sadie still grappling for the gun. DJ climbed on top of Lloyd, pulling back his fist to hit the man in the face so hard it knocked his head back, banging it on the worn wood floor. For a moment, he appeared to pass out. She managed to get the gun away. As she pointed it at Lloyd's head, her hands trembling, she saw the blood. Just as she'd feared, DJ had been hit.

Lloyd blinked and tried to rise. "Don't tempt me," she said to Lloyd over the pandemonium that had broken out in the room.

"Everyone just settle down," the cowboy in the doorway yelled. "I'm Buck Crawford. I'm a private investigator looking for DJ Diamond. I'm here on behalf of his family. I'm not interested in whatever else is happening here."

A RESTLESS QUIET fell over the room. DJ pushed his forearm against Lloyd's throat as he took the gun from Sadie and pressed it into the man's side. He met Sadie's gaze. "Are you all right?"

She nodded, but he could tell that she was scared. He followed her widened gaze to his left arm, surprised to see that his shirt a few inches above his elbow was soaked with blood. His blood. He hadn't realized he'd been winged.

"We're going to get up," he said loud enough that the cowboy PI in the doorway could hear. He kept the gun against Lloyd's ribs as the three of them rose to their feet, Sadie next to him. She pulled off the scarf from around her neck and tied it around his wound as if she was nurse Nancy. DJ was both touched and amused. The woman never ceased to amaze him.

When he looked around the room, he saw that PI Crawford and Frank seemed to be in a standoff, both with weapons drawn and pointed at the other.

"I'm going to leave," Crawford was saying from the doorway. "But I need DJ Diamond to come with me. Then the rest of you can settle whatever this is all about."

"I want none of this," Max the trucker said, and headed for the door.

Keith, who'd been sitting on the sofa counting the money, looked to Lloyd as if asking what to do. DJ shook his head at the man and jabbed Lloyd hard in the ribs. The only way they were walking out of here was if neither Lloyd nor Keith put up a fight.

Crawford moved out of the doorway to let Max leave. Bob rushed out as well.

"I'm Diamond," DJ said to the PI, happy to have an escort out of here. "But I'm not coming without Sadie." He motioned to her. She quickly picked up her purse and coat to move toward the door. DJ just hoped they weren't jumping out of the frying pan into the fire by trusting the PI. But right now, it appeared he was their best bet.

Maneuvering Lloyd over to the sofa, he jabbed the man hard in the side with the barrel end of the gun and said, "Tell Keith to give me his gun."

"You won't kill me in front of witnesses," Lloyd challenged.

"Willing to bet your life on that?" DJ said. "You hurt my girlfriend. I'd just as soon shoot you as take my next breath." He dug the barrel into Lloyd's flesh, making him wince.

"Give him your gun."

Keith carefully took his weapon from between the sofa cushions where he'd apparently hid it when the PI had burst in armed.

"Now tell him to give me the money."

"You're a dead man, Diamond," Lloyd spat, but motioned for Keith to hand over the bag. The younger man did it with obvious reluctance. "You think you can get away with this? They'll be coming for you from every direction." Lloyd smiled. "Even those closest to you have already turned on you. Nothing can save you or your girlfriend."

DJ shoved Lloyd down on the couch. He held the gun on Keith and Lloyd as he reached into the bag of money, took a handful of bills and dropped them on the table before nodding to Frank. The older man slowly lowered his weapon as if to say, "Tonight never happened."

Then DJ backed over to Sadie and the PI. He took one last look at Lloyd and Keith. They weren't Grandville's real muscle. Just as Lloyd had said, Grandville would be sending the big guns after them before they got out of Butte. Meanwhile, these two thugs would be smart to get out of town before they had to face Grandville's wrath for what had gone down here tonight.

DJ grabbed the chair at the end of the table as the three of them walked out of the room. He closed the door, sticking the chair under the knob. It wouldn't keep the men from getting out, but it would slow them down.

Once outside in the alley, DJ breathed in the cold December night air. They'd dodged a bullet. Almost, he thought as he looked down at his arm and the blood-soaked scarf tied around it. With his uninjured arm, he pulled Sadie to him. She wrapped her arms around his waist, leaning into him, as they walked down the alley. He could feel her trembling. Or maybe it was him who was shaking inside. He was back in Butte and it was as if he'd never left.

"My truck is just up the street," the PI said. "I work for Colt Brothers Investigation out of Lonesome. We need to talk."

THROUGH THE FALLING SNOW, Buck saw that Titus Grandville's car was gone from where it had been parked earlier. He must have left when he thought his two men had everything under control. Or when the gunplay started. Buck hadn't heard him leave, but then again, he'd been busy.

He still couldn't believe they'd gotten out of that mess back there alive. Worse, he didn't know which side of the law Ansley's twin was on or what he'd just helped him do. All he knew was that Titus Grandville was up to his neck in this—and so was DJ Diamond.

"I appreciate what you did back there," DJ said. "But right now, you don't want to be anywhere near the two of us. When those two back there report to their boss—"

"Titus Grandville." DJ shot him a surprised look. "I followed him to the game earlier. I'm pretty sure he already knows what went down tonight and that's why he's taken off. As far as being involved, I'm already more involved than you know. You owe me at least time to explain why I've been looking for you. My truck's down here. Let's get out of the snowstorm."

"You said you work for DJ's family?" Sadie asked once she climbed in the front of the crew cab and DJ got in the back out of the weather. Buck started the engine, letting it run as the heater warmed up the car. The temperature hovered around zero as the storm cocooned them below a thick blanket of fresh snow.

Buck turned in his seat so he could see both DJ and Sadie. He wondered about their relationship. "What I have to tell you might come as a shock. I'm not sure how much you know about your birth." He glanced at Sadie. "Or how much you want anyone else to know. I'm sorry, we haven't officially met." He held out his hand to her. "I'm—"

"Buck Crawford." She smiled. "I'm Sadie Montclair." She looked at DJ. "If he'd just as soon I not hear what it is you have to tell him—"

"No, she stays," DJ said as he looked from her to the PI. He'd kept so much of himself from the rest of the world, maybe especially Sadie because he hadn't wanted her to think the worst of him. But all that had changed tonight when he'd almost gotten her killed. He was still shaken at how close he'd come to losing her.

"Anything you have to say to me you can say in front of her," he said, his voice cracking as he shifted his gaze back to her and swallowed the lump that had risen in his throat. They had to make this quick. If the PI was right and Grandville already knew what had gone down here tonight, he would be sending more of his men for them.

"I'll give you the abbreviated version," the PI said, no doubt seeing how anxious he was. "About thirty years ago your mother was pregnant with twins, a girl and a boy. It was a rough delivery. She believed that you both had died. But you'd both been given away by a woman who thought she was doing the best thing for the two of you. I'm here on behalf of your twin sister, who is getting married at the end of this week. She didn't know about you until recently. Actually, she didn't know that the people who raised her weren't really her biological parents. Once she found out, she wouldn't stop until she found her birth mother. That's when she found out that she had a twin brother. I believe you are that missing twin."

DJ scoffed. Did he believe any of this? It sounded like a con. "That's quite a story."

"We won't know for sure until we get your DNA, but you look a lot like Ansley. The dark hair, the blue eyes… It's kind of incredible."

Incredible, DJ thought, feeling like he needed to ask what's the hitch. "So what's in it for you if I'm this missing twin?"

"I don't blame you for being suspicious. Other than finding my future bride's brother for her, I'm hoping you'll be at our wedding."

DJ felt his eyebrows shoot up as Crawford nodded.

"Ansley Brookshire is my fiancée."

"Brookshire?" That was a name he'd heard. It was right up there with Grandville—just not as old money. "Sorry if I'm having trouble believing this."

The PI pulled out his cell and flipped through the photos for a moment before handing the phone over to him. DJ stared down at the pretty woman with the dark hair and familiar blue eyes. His heart raced. Could this be true? "Other than I resemble her, what makes you think I'm the twin?"

"I've followed a trail from the birth mother to here," Crawford said. "I found your growth chart out at Charley Diamond's ranch. I'm pretty sure Darrow Grandville left you out there. It's a long story, but the sooner we get a DNA test the sooner we'll know for sure."

"If you're telling me that a Grandville was my father—"

"No," Buck said with a shake of his head. "If you're who I think you are, then your father is Del Ransom Colt, a former rodeo bull rider and the man who started Colt Investigations in Lonesome."

All DJ could think was that he couldn't trust this. Trust had always been an issue with him. Until he met Sadie. But hadn't he always wondered who he was, how he'd been left out at the ranch with Charley and if anyone had ever wanted him? He looked at Sadie as he handed her the phone with the picture of the young woman who could be his twin.

She glanced at the photo, her eyes widening in

the same shock he'd felt. Maybe it *was* possible, but the timing couldn't have been worse.

A set of headlights bled through the falling snow that had accumulated on the windshield.

"All this is interesting, but we really need to get out of here," DJ said. "Grandville's men are going to be looking for us." He waited until the vehicle coming toward them passed before he started to open his door. "I'm going to have to get back to you."

BUCK COULDN'T FIND Ansley's twin only to have him disappear again. "Look, I can see that you're in some kind of trouble," he said quickly. "Let me help you." He pulled out his business card with his cell phone number on it.

"Sorry, but you can't help," DJ said as he reluctantly took the business card and handed back Buck's phone. "A friend of mine is in danger. I have to get to her before they do."

"You might want to get some medical attention for that wound first," Buck said.

"I can see to it," Sadie said like a woman who'd done her share of patching up gunshot wounds. Buck had to wonder who this woman was and just how much trouble the two of them were in. But if Titus Grandville was involved, it was dangerous.

"I could help you more if you told me why Titus Grandville is after you—and your friend. If it's money, maybe I can—"

"It's more than money," DJ said. "But thanks for

the offer. With me and Grandville it's apparently personal. My…friend's husband owes Titus money. He's pressuring her. I've got her hidden. After what went down tonight, I'm afraid of what they'll do to her if they find her, and I have no doubt that they are looking for her."

"DJ, if you go to her now, you'll lead them right to her," Buck said quickly. "I can keep all of you safe if you come back to Lonesome with me." He saw the answer and quickly added, "At least let me keep your friend safe until this is over. You can trust me."

DJ shook his head. He was clearly someone who'd been taking care of himself for so long that he was suspicious of help. But before he could decline the offer, the woman spoke.

"He's right. If you go to Keira now, you'll just be putting her in danger," she said, reaching back to take DJ's hand. "I trust him. He just saved us back there."

Keira. The name of the other child from the ranch. Buck could see that DJ was having a hard time trusting him. But there was something between these two, the woman he called Sadie and DJ himself. Apparently, DJ did trust her, because Buck saw him weaken.

DJ LOOKED AT SADIE, felt that lump form again in his throat as she nodded her encouragement. He'd almost gotten her killed tonight. He should have trusted her and aborted when she'd signaled for him to. But he hadn't. He'd been so sure he knew what he was doing. He'd trusted only a few people in his life. He realized that if there was one person he trusted with his life, it was Sadie. But did he dare risk Keira's life by trusting this PI?

He looked at Buck Crawford, reminding himself that Sadie was right—the man had just saved their lives back there. But it was Sadie's trust in the man that made him decide. "Her name's Keira Cross. She's in Whitehall at the Rice Motel. Tell her I sent you. She won't believe you, so you'll have to show her this."

He dug in his pocket and pulled out the tiny, tarnished gold bracelet with his initials on it. For a moment all he could do was rub his thumb over the *DJ* engraved in the gold. He'd had it from as far back as he could remember. It was why they'd called him DJ at the ranch.

He'd carried it for luck. He didn't even know who'd given it to him—just that it had been his talisman. He handed it to the PI. "Keira means a lot to me."

Crawford nodded as he took the bracelet and pocketed it. "I'll make sure she's safe." He handed his phone back to DJ. "Put your number in there. I'll call you when I have her." DJ took the phone again and keyed in his number, hoping he wasn't making a mistake. "The wedding is next Saturday."

DJ shook his head as he handed the phone back. "You aren't even sure I'm your future bride's missing twin."

"I'm not much of a gambler, but I'd put all my

money on it. Next Saturday. It would mean everything to Ansley and me if you were there."

"Aren't you worried that I'm a wanted criminal who could be behind bars by then?" DJ asked, amazed by this PI.

"I'm a pretty good judge of character. Also, I know a good bail bondsman," Crawford told him. "I'll call you the minute I have Keira safe."

Chapter Eleven

"Can you ever forgive me?" DJ asked as he started the SUV's engine without looking at Sadie, and waited for the wipers to clear the windshield. He heard her buckle her seatbelt before she finally spoke.

"There's nothing to forgive," she said, her voice sounding hoarse.

His gaze swung to hers in disbelief. "I almost got you killed!"

"I'm fine." She wasn't. He could hear in her voice the scratchy sound of her bruised throat. It had to hurt since he could see the bruised area where Lloyd had held her too tightly. He gripped the wheel until his fingers turned white just thinking about Lloyd with his arm around her neck cutting off her air. "I should have listened to you and gotten out of there before—"

"I thought it was Frank. I saw his ankle holster and gun right after I sat down. He looked like former military or an ex-cop. I panicked."

DJ shook his head. "It doesn't matter. I was wrong.

You went with your instincts, and they were right. I'm so sorry."

"You have nothing to be sorry for."

He shifted the SUV into Drive and started down the street. "How can you even say that? If I had listened to you, we would have gotten out of there before Lloyd grabbed you."

"Would we have? I really doubt they were going to let us just walk out."

DJ didn't argue the point as he took a road out of Butte. It didn't matter which way he headed as long as it was out of town. "I thought I knew what I was doing. You were right. I was too personally involved. I believed that Grandville wanted his money bad enough that he'd let me win enough to pay him off. I underestimated him. I doubt now it was ever about the money."

Out of the corner of his eye, he saw Sadie nod. "Do the two of you have a history?"

"Back when we were kids," he said. "Just a couple of brief occurrences when our paths crossed. He was the rich kid. I was nobody. But I must have made an impression on him."

"You do have that ability," she agreed, and he saw her smile. "Do you think he might have used Keira to get you back in Montana?"

So like her to cut to the heart of it. For a moment, he couldn't answer. The thought hurt too bad. He refused to believe the kid he thought of as his little sister would betray him. "I'll ask her when I see her."

His words kind of hung in the air. Sadie didn't say anything. The only sound was the swish of the windshield wipers as he drove through the falling snow. He saw that he was headed for Helena. He knew he was waiting to hear from Crawford and simply driving to stay one step ahead of the men after them.

It didn't matter what town they reached as long as it had an airport, where he planned to put Sadie on a plane home. It had been a mistake calling her and getting her up here. He'd selfishly wanted her with him, he could admit now. He hadn't really needed her. He'd been right about one thing, though…it had been their last game. He'd almost gotten her killed for nothing.

"You know that I have to finish this."

Sadie said nothing for a few moments. "What exactly is this?"

"I thought I was just coming back here to pay off Grandville and free Keira from the debt and her no-account husband. Now I'm not sure what this is. All I know is I never should have gotten you involved."

THE DRIVE TO Whitehall took longer than Buck had expected because of the storm. He didn't think he'd been followed, but he'd still taken precautions just in case. The one thing he couldn't let happen was leading Grandville's thugs straight to Keira Cross's motel room. He'd gotten DJ Diamond to trust him. Now Buck just had to prove that his trust had been warranted. It was the only way he was going to get the missing twin to his and Ansley's wedding.

He tried not to worry about DJ and Sadie or speculate on just how much trouble the two were in with the Grandvilles. DJ was the missing twin. Didn't the bracelet prove it? But how to keep him alive was the problem. There was nothing he could do about that—at least not at the moment. Once he had Keira and knew she was safe…

The snow was falling harder as he pulled up in front of the Rice Motel in Whitehall. It was still dark, the hour late. The crack of dawn wasn't that far away. For a moment he just sat in his pickup watching the snow, watching the parking lot, hoping she was inside number nine and that he would soon be calling DJ with the good news.

Still, he couldn't help being a little leery. This felt almost too easy. That and the one man's words back in Butte about DJ not being able to trust those closest to him. He didn't see anyone else in the parking lot and there were only a couple of cars in front of two of the other motel rooms. On the surface, everything looked fine.

Still, as he got out of the pickup, he felt the hair spike on the back of his neck. He moved quickly to the motel unit door and knocked. No answer. He knocked again, then he tried the knob, his anxiety growing. The knob turned in his hand and with just a little push, the door swung open.

"Keira?" he called again. "Keira?" It was pitch-black inside the room, but as his eyes began to focus, he could see that there was someone in the bed. She was either a sound sleeper or... He raised his voice. "Keira?" He took a step in, his heart in his throat for fear that Grandville's men had already gotten to her.

Buck heard movement off to his right side. He turned, but not quickly enough. He caught a glimpse of Titus Grandville an instant before he was struck with something hard and cold. He staggered and went down hard.

AFTER DRIVING NORTH toward Helena and the airport there, DJ tried Keira's cell. He couldn't risk the Butte airport. He'd already decided that he would get the PI to bring Keira to him. Somehow, he'd talk her into going to Florida with him. The Grandvilles might run Butte, their tentacles stretching even into the states around them, but they wouldn't come after them in Florida. If she wouldn't go, he'd know that she still loved Luca and had no intention of leaving him.

The call went straight to voicemail—just as it had earlier. Had trusting the PI been a mistake? Or had the Grandvilles been waiting for Crawford? If so, then they already had Keira. He tried Crawford. The call went to voicemail. Disconnecting, he felt worry bore deep into him. He told himself that he should have heard something by now.

"She could have stepped out to get something to

eat," Sadie said, no doubt seeing his concern. She didn't sound any more convinced than he was.

He'd left a message for her to call, but his instincts told him she wasn't going to because she either couldn't or wouldn't. He'd been set up tonight at the poker game. Grandville had been two steps ahead of him the whole time. Keith and Lloyd had been low-rung thugs. Now Grandville would send his A-team after them, the men Keira had told him about, Butch Lamar and Rafe Westfall. Paying Grandville off was no longer an option. Maybe it never had been.

He'd had a bad feeling from the moment things had gone south at the poker game. Something was at play here, something that had him off-balance. He kept thinking about what Lloyd had hinted at, something about those closest to him turning on him. There was only one meaning he could get from that.

Keira.

If he couldn't trust her, Luca Cross was to blame, he told himself. Hadn't he worried that Keira was still in love with him, that she would go back to him, that he would get in trouble again? He told himself he shouldn't have ever let her marry the man, like he could have stopped her.

But even as he thought it, he knew he couldn't blame Luca. Keira had taken to life on the ranch even as a young girl, fascinated with the criminals who came and went. He'd caught her learning sleight of hand tricks by one of the cons when she was five. She'd been good at it. He'd seen the pride in her eyes.

"It's in her genes," Charley had always said with a laugh. "She was born to this life. As much as we don't want to be anything like our biological parents, we are part of that gene stew. Just need to make the best of the hand you've drawn. Remember that, DJ. Accept who you are."

He thought he had, even though he hadn't known his gene pool. But he had wanted to believe it didn't have to be Keira's future. He'd done his best to protect her, but he'd only been a boy himself back on the ranch. After that, he hadn't seen her much because he'd been trying to stay alive and not starve.

Thinking about his own biological stew, he wondered about this twin sister, if he really was her twin. Ansley Brookshire. She'd certainly landed in the lap of luxury, he thought uncharitably. By now she knew that if DJ was her twin, they weren't in the same league—not by a long shot. Maybe she would change her mind about meeting him—let alone having him stand up with her at her wedding. He wouldn't blame her if she did.

As Charley used to say, "It's all in the cards and how you play them." Isn't that what worried him? DJ thought. Was Keira in the game?

He refused to believe it. He called again and this time left a message. "Where are you?"

BUCK OPENED HIS eyes to darkness. For a moment, he didn't remember anything—especially where he was. On the floor in a motel room. It took him a moment to adjust to the light coming through the partially cracked blinds. As his memory returned, he rolled over so he could see the bed. Empty. He pushed himself up into a sitting position, his head a little clearer.

He was surprised to realize that his gun was still in his holster. How long had he been out? He checked for his phone. Still in his coat pocket. He hadn't been out that long even though it was now daylight outside—and still snowing, and Keira was gone. He couldn't be sure she'd even been the body he'd seen covered in the bed.

The only thing he knew for sure was that he had a bump on the side of his head the size of a walnut. Nor was there any doubt that Titus Grandville was behind this. He hoped he'd get the chance to return the favor.

As he felt steadier, he got to his feet. Turning on a light, he checked out the motel room. No sign of a struggle. No blood. He checked the bed. It had been slept in, but also no blood. Keira had either been taken—or had walked out on her own.

But whoever had hit him had been expecting company. Had they thought it would be DJ? They must have been disappointed.

He peeked out at the parking lot. His truck was still right outside, but the rest of the parking lot was now empty. The two vehicles he'd seen earlier were gone. Either they had been early-rising guests, or they'd been Grandville's men.

As he started to turn out the light and leave, he felt something in his other coat pocket. He carefully pulled it out. The unsealed envelope had *To DJ* written on the outside.

Buck frowned as he opened the flap and quickly read the contents. Pulling out his phone, he called DJ.

DJ HAD DRIVEN as far as Helena last night. They'd parked in a Walmart lot, sleeping in the back of the SUV. This morning, he and Sadie had eaten breakfast at a local truck stop. Now, not even a mile from the airport, he knew he had to make a decision. He hadn't heard from either Keira or the PI. Both could be dead, although he doubted Grandville would kill Keira—not until he got whatever it was he wanted out of DJ.

Crawford was another story. He'd trusted the man, still did because Sadie did. He just hoped he hadn't gotten the man killed. He was mentally kicking himself for involving other people in this when his phone rang.

With a wave of both concern and relief, he saw it was PI Buck Crawford. He picked up. "Was my sister there?" he asked.

"No."

He listened as the PI told him what had happened when he'd reached the motel room. The news didn't come as a surprise. He'd already figured that Grandville's men had found her. "Are you all right?"

"I'll live," Crawford said. "But apparently she left you a note."

He listened as Crawford read: *"I saw them look-*

ing for me in town. I barely got away. I have no choice. I'm going to meet Luca up at Charley Diamond's cabin in the mountains north of Lonesome.

Thank you for trying to help me, but I know things didn't go well up in Butte or you would have been back by now. Luca and I are going to head for Alaska. It's only a matter of time before Grandville comes looking for us if we stay here.'"

Keira, no, DJ thought. She was making a huge mistake. He had to stop her, or she'd be running the rest of her life. "Any chance she left directions to the cabin?"

Silence, then Crawford said, "She did." What he didn't say, but DJ heard, were the words "almost as if she was hoping you'd go to the cabin to try to stop her." The PI continued reading. *"'I'd love to see you before we leave. In case you forgot where Charley's cabin is, here's the directions. If we miss each other, thank you again for everything.'"*

"DJ, you have to wonder why she'd leave you the directions to the cabin," Crawford said. "Are you sure you can trust her?"

He felt anger boil up inside him. "She's been like a little sister to me from the time she was just a toddler," he snapped. "Just give me the directions."

Again there was that slight hesitation before the PI read the directions.

"Thanks. Send me a bill," DJ said, hating that Crawford was thinking the same thing he was. If he went to Charley's old cabin outside of Lonesome, he could be walking into a trap—a trap set by someone he loved and thought he could trust with his life.

"You already know it isn't money I want," Crawford said. "Saturday at the only white church in Lonesome. Four o'clock."

He disconnected. He could feel Sadie's gaze on him and see the recrimination in her expression. The PI had done him a favor, gotten his head bashed in, and this was the way DJ repaid it. Of course she'd heard the entire conversation in the confines of the SUV. He could see that she agreed with the PI. Going up to the cabin was a mistake, maybe the last one he'd ever make.

But when she spoke, it was only to say, "So we're going up into the mountains to your uncle's cabin to meet her."

"Not *we*. Just me. I should never have gotten you involved in this. I'm putting you on the next plane to Florida."

"You know that isn't going to happen. I'm going with you because clearly you're determined to see her. You don't believe that she would turn on you and you could be right."

He held her gaze, but words stuck in his throat. He probably wasn't right; that's what hurt. Keira had betrayed him. He knew it and yet he refused to believe it until he heard it from her. And by then, it would be too late.

"I have to know," DJ said, fearing that the bond he and Keira had was never as strong as he'd thought.

It was something he didn't want to think about right now. "I also have to try to save her if I can. Grandville will never let her go now."

SADIE FELT HER heart break for him. He and Keira weren't really brother and sister, but it didn't matter to DJ if they were blood or not. Some bonds were even stronger.

She could understand his loyalty and love for this girl he'd taken under his wing from an early age. Two children thrown together under strange if not terrifying circumstances. She thought of her own childhood. She'd been alone in an adult world that she knew wasn't normal. Her parents dead after their small private plane had crashed. If it hadn't been for her godfather, who knows what would have happened to her.

Ezra Montclair had taken her in, raised her, taught her the business as if she were the heir to his kingdom. She'd been all alone in that adult world. She would have loved to have another child to be there with her, let alone to watch her back. She'd learned to navigate through the many men who came to see her godfather. She'd learned to be invisible, to listen and learn, to not be a child.

"I envy the relationship you had with her," Sadie said at last. "I would have loved a big brother watching over me like you have Keira."

He said nothing, looking sick for fear he was wrong about her. Worse, that Keira had lied about the debt owed to the Grandvilles knowing he would come back to Montana to help her. If she'd deceived him, she had to know what Titus Grandville would do to DJ. She couldn't be that naive.

"I needed her as much as she needed me," he said. "She gave me a purpose."

Like paying off Uncle Charley's debt, she thought. Now that debt was paid. Keira in need had become his new purpose. But what after that? she wondered, realizing how driven DJ had been. First it had been just the fight to survive in the world he'd found himself in. Later, it was repaying even a dcad Charley for giving him a home, an occupation, a way to survive once he was on his own.

She realized that she and DJ weren't all that different. Both Charley and her godfather had taught them well. They were survivors.

Chapter Twelve

DJ made his decision. "I need you to go back to Florida." She started to speak, but he stopped her. "Sadie, I'm begging you. I'll take you to the airport so you can catch a flight home. It has to be this way. *Please*."

She shook her head, raising a hand and cutting him off. "I'm not letting you do this alone. You're wounded and you need me. We're partners, remember?"

He shook his head. "That's over. Your godfather and I are square. You and I are square, aren't we?" He held her gaze and saw something so soft and vulnerable that he had to look away. They were so much more than that, he thought as his heart lifted, then fell. Hadn't he wanted desperately to be with this woman—and not just as business partners. Now that they had a chance to be together… "You know I might be walking into a trap that could get me killed."

"Get us killed," she corrected. "But we stand a better chance together, always have. We check out the cabin. If it looks like a setup…" She drew his gaze back to her. "We walk away. Together. One last game. If we realize we can't win it, we throw in our cards and fold. There is no shame in walking away when the odds are against you."

He knew what she was saying. It didn't have to end this way. He had a choice. They had a choice. If he forced her on the plane… His heart ached at the thought that it would be over for them even if Keira hadn't betrayed him, even if he lived to tell about it. He couldn't imagine *never* seeing Sadie again. She would be walking away with a huge chunk of his heart he hadn't even realized he'd given her. But it would kill him if he got her hurt any more than he already had.

"I need to re-bandage that wound," she said as if the discussion was over. For her it was. "If you don't take me with you, I'll rent my own SUV," she said as if reading his mind. "I heard the directions to the cabin. I'm not leaving you, DJ. Not when you need me more than you ever have before. So don't even think about driving off and leaving me the first time I'm out of your sight."

He'd just been planning that exact thing. The thought made him sick inside that he would stoop to tricking her, since he'd always tried to be honest with her. She would go up to the cabin on her own. That kind of loyalty made the thought of Keira betraying him all the more painful. He saw her look around the SUV.

"Do you know what happened to the scarf I had tied on your wound?" she asked.

"I'm sorry. I must have lost it."

"It's not important." She met his gaze. "Keeping you alive is, though."

He couldn't take his eyes off her. The woman had always amazed him, but never as much as she did right now. Yet he couldn't help thinking that she'd picked the wrong horse to put her money on. "You seem to have some fool idea that you can save me from myself. What if you can't, Sadie? What if I've been a lost cause all along?"

She shook her head. "You have a twin sister who'll be standing at the altar soon waiting for her twin brother. You're going to show up and not let her down or die trying. She needs you and you just might need her and the family she's offering you. Now let me see your arm."

Buck called James back at Colt Brothers Investigation the minute he got off the phone with DJ. He quickly told him everything that had happened.

"The man you believe to be Ansley's twin is headed up in the mountains to confront a woman he grew up with and is probably walking into a trap?" James asked. "What is wrong with him?"

"Apparently, DJ and this young woman, Keira, were raised together there on the ranch. He considers her his sister. He doesn't believe she would betray him."

"You told him he might have a twin sister, a real sister by blood?"

"I think he's worried it's a scam," Buck said. "You have to understand, he isn't very trusting and given the way he grew up, I get it. I'm on my way back to Lonesome. I have a scarf I found in my pickup with his blood on it. I'm hoping Willie can get us a DNA sample from it to confirm that DJ Diamond is Ansley's lost brother. He looks way too much like her not to be. Stubborn to a fault like her, too. Also I followed a trail from Lonesome and the woman who sold the babies to DJ Diamond. It's too much of a coincidence for him not to be the missing twin. The real kicker, though, is that he had the gold bracelet his birth mother had made for him with the initials DJ on it. I get the feeling it's his talisman, his good-luck charm. He's the real deal."

"Where are you headed now?" James asked as if he already suspected Buck's next move.

"As soon as I get back to Lonesome, I'm going to hook up to my snowmobile trailer and head up into the mountains. Keira Diamond Cross left directions to the cabin where she said she'd be waiting. DJ will be coming from the west side of the mountains. I plan to beat him to the cabin. I can't let him walk into a trap."

"Even without the blizzard, the freezing temps and killers possibly waiting at this cabin?"

"I can't let Ansley down." It was more than that.

He liked DJ Diamond. He didn't want to see anything happen to him or to the woman with him.

"Getting yourself killed would be much worse than not having her brother at her wedding," James said. "There would be no wedding without you. That's why I'm going with you."

"Me, too," Tommy said, making Buck realize that he'd been on speaker.

"You have a pregnant wife," both Buck and James said at the same time.

"She's not due for a month," Tommy protested. "Stop by my place with the trailer. We'll throw on a couple more snowmobiles. Safety in numbers, you know."

Buck chuckled. "I'm on my way. But one more thing. DJ has a woman with him, Sadie Montclair. See what you can find out about her."

SADIE CHECKED DJ'S WOUND, cleaned and bandaged his upper arm against his protests that it was just a flesh wound. It had been a clean shot, tearing through skin and flesh and fortunately missing the bone. It had to be painful, but he didn't show it. So like DJ, she thought. The man was the strongest, most determined man she'd ever known. He was also the kindest and surprisingly, the gentlest. His heart was so big, which she knew was why he was in so much emotional pain over Keira. The one thing he wasn't was a lost cause, no matter what he thought. She hoped she could prove that to him before it was too late.

The weather report they heard on the radio was dire. It was still blizzarding across the state. Residents were advised not to travel except in cases of an emergency. Sadie listened to the steady clack of the windshield wipers. They were doing their best but seeming to struggle to keep up. Because of the falling snow and the wind whipping it, visibility was only a matter of yards.

DJ seemed oblivious to the blizzard and the snow-covered road. She watched him drive, his strong hands on the wheel, his expression calm, maybe too calm, his amazing blue eyes intent on what road he could see ahead.

"Florida didn't seem to diminish your winter driving skills," she said, hating that the whirling snow outside the cab was making her nervous. She was born and raised in Florida. She hadn't even seen snow until she was in her teens. She'd never been in a storm like this one. How could something so beautiful be so treacherous?

"Driving in the snow is like falling off a bike," he said.

"I believe the expression is like riding a bike," she corrected, playing along.

He grinned over at her for a second. "We'll be fine. You trust me, don't you?"

She knew he meant more than with his driving in this storm. "I trust you with my life."

He shook his head almost ruefully. "That's what worries me."

A Christmas song came on the radio. He reached over and turned it off.

"What do you have against Christmas?" she asked, feeling a need to fill the silence, but also wanting to know more about this man. All the hours she'd spent with him and yet she knew little of his early life at Charley Diamond's ranch.

"Nothing against Christmas. Just never was something we celebrated at the ranch. Charley said it was a scam." DJ laughed. "He said a lot of things were a scam. He should know."

She laughed. "See, we have even more in common. My godfather didn't celebrate holidays either. Said they were businessmen's trick to play on people's emotions so they felt guilty if they didn't spend more money than they had. I never cared about the present part of Christmas."

For a moment, she watched snow flying around them in a dizzying blur. "But I did love the lights and the decorations. I always felt that there was something special about the season beyond all the commercialism. We were far from a religious family, but there was something spiritual that I felt at Christmas." She fell silent before adding with a laugh, "I always wanted a real Christmas tree. Did you have a Christmas tree at the ranch?"

"No."

Sadie felt him turn toward her for a second before going back to his driving.

After a few minutes, she realized she wasn't getting any more out of him. They drove through the whiteout with only the clack of the wipers and the hum of the heater. She kept losing sight of the road ahead. She felt as if they were driving into a wall of white with no idea of what was on the other side. The snow had a claustrophobic quality, no longer as beautiful as she'd first thought. It now felt dangerous.

The weather report on the radio continued to get worse. Many of the highways were closed due to a lack of visibility. The snow kept getting deeper on the highway. She realized that she couldn't remember the last time she'd seen a car go by, let alone a snowplow.

Through a break in the whirling snow, she saw a sign. DJ slowed and turned onto a narrower road. This one led up higher into the mountains. The snow quickly got deeper. The SUV broke through the drifts that the wind had sculpted, sending a shower of white flakes up over the windshield.

Sadie was relieved that DJ seemed to know how to maneuver in the deep snow filling the narrow road. That wasn't what had her worried, though. It was why he was driving in a blizzard when roads were closing, drivers were told to stay home, plows couldn't keep up. This part of the state was closing down and yet DJ kept going as if racing toward his destiny.

She'd seen determination in him many times before, but not like this. She could only hope that Keira had been telling the truth. She and her husband might already be on their way to Alaska. What would DJ do if he missed them? Would that be enough proof that Keira hadn't betrayed him?

The road wound up the mountain. The wind was reduced with the thick pines on each side of the road so the snow wasn't as drifted. They kept climbing. Sadie remembered being in awe of the winter wonderland DJ had brought her to. Now it had a lethal quality that unnerved her. It was bad enough that they were probably driving into a trap—and that's if they survived the blizzard and the drive up this mountain.

You trust me, don't you? DJ had asked.

I trust you with my life.

"It should be right up here," DJ said as they topped a small hill and he turned up an even more narrow road. He started up it. They hadn't gone far when she heard a spinning sound as the tires fought to find traction—and failed.

The SUV came to a stop. DJ tried to get it going again, but the whine of the tires told her that they weren't going any farther. DJ backed up and made a run at the hill. The same thing happened: tires spun, no traction. Only this time, the pickup slid off the road, and the driver's side dropped into what appeared to be a narrow ditch—not that she could tell with the snow so deep.

"Stay here." He jumped out, leaving the engine running, the heater cranked. He was out of the SUV, cold rushing in as he exited, then he disappeared into the storm. Sadie hugged herself and waited, not sure where he had gone. To see how stuck they were? But when he didn't return, she began to worry. What if something happened and he didn't come back? The thought raced past, kicking up her pulse and making her stomach churn. She was completely out of her element. How long could she survive out here? She quickly shoved the thought away. DJ would come back. If he could.

She checked to see how much gas they had. Less than half a tank. She reached over and turned the key. The engine stopped and so did the heater. An eerie, deafening quiet filled the vehicle. She felt the cold surround the SUV and begin making its way in. Moments ago, it had been almost too warm. She shivered, realizing she wouldn't survive long if DJ didn't make it back.

The air inside the truck was getting colder by the second. How long had she been sitting here? How long had DJ been gone?

She tried to see outside. The wind would occasionally part the falling snow enough that she could see pine trees. Had they reached the cabin where he was to meet Keira? Surely he wouldn't have gone in to face Keira alone knowing he could be walking into a trap! She should have jumped out and gone with him, but he hadn't given her a chance.

But even as she thought it, she knew that was exactly what he would do to protect her. She buttoned up her coat and reached for her scarf before she remembered that she'd used it to put over DJ's wound and he'd lost it somewhere. She must not have tied it tight enough.

She dressed as warmly as she could manage; still, she hesitated. Should she go after him? She wasn't even sure which way he'd gone or if this was the road to the cabin. Leaving the pickup seemed like a bad idea since the alternative was to go out into the snow and cold. Snow had accumulated on the windshield. Soon she wouldn't be able to see out.

She reached for the door handle and stopped. Through a break in the falling snow, she caught movement. She held her breath, unsure what was up here in these woods. Animal? Or human?

Her heart bumped hard against her ribs as DJ appeared out of the storm. Relief made her weak for a moment as he opened the door and climbed in.

For a startled moment, she didn't recognize him with his hair and coat covered with snow. Flakes clung to his long dark lashes. "Are we— Is this—"

He must have seen her relief and her fear. "Sorry, I didn't mean to leave you alone for so long. Charley's cabin is on up the road about halfway up the mountain."

"Keira?"

He shook his head. "But someone's been here. There is food and firewood. I found a branding iron with the Diamond Deluxe, a diamond shape with a D inside. I hurried up and built a fire so it would be warmer for you once we climb up the mountainside. It's a pretty good hike up."

"No problem," she said without hesitation. Anywhere was better after sitting here thinking the worst might have happened.

"We'll be warm and dry. I saw older tracks in the snow. I might have already missed her. Otherwise…"

Otherwise, she could be coming once the storm passed, he didn't say, but she knew what he meant. He pulled the SUV key and met her gaze. "Don't worry. I've got everything covered."

She'd heard these words before, so they didn't give her much assurance. The thing about DJ Diamond, though, was when things went south, he always came up with a backup plan. Whether he'd thought of it before things went bad or not was debatable. But he'd always managed to save them. She just hoped he hadn't met his match this time as she climbed out into the Montana blizzard.

BUCK HEARD THE relief in Ainsley's voice the moment she answered the phone. "Are you all right? I've been so worried about you."

"I'm fine. I'm sorry I haven't called sooner." There was no way he was getting into everything that had happened since he'd last seen her. Eventually, Ansley would know most of it.

"Did you find him?" Her voice cracked. He could hear the hope and felt his heart break for her. He'd wanted so badly to have good news for her.

"I think I've found him, but we won't know for sure until we get the DNA results."

"That's wonderful news," she cried. She sounded so relieved. She really did have her heart set on him giving her away at the wedding. He wished he could have talked her into putting off the ceremony until spring, but she'd wanted a Christmas wedding and he would give her anything.

He told her what he'd learned and about going out to the Diamond Deluxe Ranch and what he'd found out there.

"His name is DJ Diamond?" she said. "It has to be him if he had the gold bracelet our mother had made for him. And he grew up on a ranch, that's great."

He didn't know how to tell her. It was one reason he hadn't called until now. He'd put it off, telling himself he wanted to be sure that DJ Diamond was indeed her twin. But the truth was he didn't know how to tell her about the life her twin might have lived.

"It wasn't that kind of ranch," he told her now. They were about to start their lives together. He didn't want there to be any lies between them. She needed to know the truth, as hard as it was going to be to tell her—let alone for her to hear. He told her about everything that he'd learned. For a moment there was only silence on the line. "Ainsley, are you there?"

"You're saying he's a criminal?"

"No. Maybe. I'm not sure. He was raised by an

uncle who was a conman who apparently taught him everything he knows. From what I can tell he makes his living gambling."

"What aren't you telling me, Buck?"

He sighed. "Right now DJ's on the run after a poker game went badly. He has a friend who's in trouble and he's determined to save her. James, Tommy and I are going after him, but we aren't the only ones anxious to catch up to him and this friend of his he grew up with. There are some powerful men also after him. I don't want to upset you, but I think we should postpone the wedding."

Chapter Thirteen

On the climb up the mountainside to the cabin, DJ mentally kicked himself. Sadie should be winging her way to the sunny shores of Florida right now—not trudging through thigh-high snow with him. He should have been more insistent. As if that would have changed her mind. He imagined himself physically putting her on a plane home. That was just as ridiculous as thinking he could make her do anything she didn't want to do.

But bringing her up here… A gust of wind whirled fresh snow around him. He caught a glimpse of the cabin above them almost hidden in the tall pines.

"A little longer and we'll be there," he said to her as he stopped to let them both catch their breath. They were used to Florida and sea level. He looked at her, trying to gauge how she was doing—and not just from the climb. He'd gotten her into this, something he deeply regretted. It was bad enough that he'd been possibly tricked into coming back here—let alone that he'd dragged Sadie into it. He couldn't bear the thought that Keira had purposely drawn him back to Montana on a lie so that Grandville could get retribution for some old grudge.

Pushing the nagging thought away, he said, "You doing okay?"

"I'm good," she said, and flashed him a smile. It wasn't one of her brilliant, knock-a-man-for-a-loop smiles. This one was part worry, part sympathy. He wanted to tell her that he'd be fine no matter what he found out, but he couldn't lie to her because she would see right through it. If Keira had turned on him… He hated to think of the pain it would cause. That's if she didn't get him killed.

"It's not far now," he said.

"Lead the way, partner."

A few minutes later, they waded through the drifted snow up onto the porch. As he opened the front door of the cabin, he gave a slight bow and waved her inside. He had no idea how long they would be here. At least until the storm passed. Where was Keira? Had she gotten caught in the storm? And what about the Grandvilles? Were they on their way as well?

Keira had chosen the perfect isolated place in the mountains for her husband to hide out. It was also a perfect place to get rid of someone. Bodies often didn't turn up for years in these woods. He tried not to think about what might happen if Keira showed up. If she was telling the truth, she and Luca might already be headed for Alaska. He realized he might never see her again if that was the case.

Or she and Luca might be planning a visit to the cabin—just waiting for him to arrive. Keira knew him. She would know that he would come to the cabin. Wasn't that why she'd left the note?

His head hurt thinking about it. He could no more see the future than flap his arms and fly. Yet his gut told him he couldn't trust her. Maybe he never could.

He looked over at Sadie, fighting the feeling that they were sitting ducks and hunting season was about to open.

SADIE STEPPED INTO the cabin and glanced around as DJ closed the door behind them. She'd caught the scent of smoke the last half dozen yards up the mountain and now welcomed just being out of the storm.

A fire crackled in an old rock fireplace against the right wall, but from what she could tell, it wasn't putting out all that much heat yet. She beat the snow off her boots before she stepped toward the heat and took in the rest of the cabin.

It was compact and open. The living area consisted of the fireplace, two upholstered chairs and a kindling box sitting open. Inside it, she could see twigs and pine cones, old newspapers and matches. Turning behind her, she saw what served as the kitchen. It consisted of a sink with a bucket under it. A propane stove and an old icebox-type refrigerator. Pots and pans hung over a small cabinet that she assumed held utensils and possibly flatware.

DJ was right. It appeared someone had been here recently. She saw a package of store-bought cookies open on the top of the cabinet. "No electricity, right?" she asked as she peeled off her gloves to hold her hands up to the fire. Her fingers ached from the cold. So did her cheeks.

"No electric, no cell service, no internet," DJ said, "but there is a root cellar–type enclosure in the back against the mountainside with canned food that isn't frozen. There is also a stove with a propane tank and a pile of dry wood under a shed roof on the side of the cabin. We won't starve and we won't freeze."

She couldn't help but smile at him as she took in the rest of the cabin. She suspected DJ often looked for a silver lining in even the darkest of clouds. There was a back door with some storage along the wall. To the right of that was a double bed taking up the corner of the room near the fireplace.

As she began to warm up, she took off her coat and dropped it into one of the chairs. She saw that they had tracked in snow, but she wasn't ready to take off her boots. Her toes were just starting to warm up.

DJ threw some more wood on the fire. She could feel the heat go to her face. Her fingers and toes began to tingle, then sting. Her cheeks ached, but she began to relax. They were safe for the moment and as he'd said, they wouldn't starve or freeze. That was enough for now.

"Not bad, huh," DJ said, and grinned.

Partners to the end, she thought. "Not bad."

He turned toward the cupboard over the stove. "Let's see what there is to eat. I don't know about you, but I'm hungry after that hike."

TITUS GRANDVILLE STARED out at the snowstorm in disgust before spinning his office chair back around to face the two men standing there with their hats in their hands.

"Let me see if I've got this straight," Titus said, trying to keep his voice down. "You lost Diamond, you lost the money and now…" His voice began to rise. "You say you can't go find him and the money and finish this because it's snowing too much?"

Rafe Westfall looked at him wide-eyed. "It's a *blizzard*. Some of the roads are closed. How are we supposed to—"

"We'll find him," Butch Lamar said. "We know Diamond's headed up into the mountains. Keira left him a note with directions to Charley's old cabin. She swears that Diamond will show. If she isn't worried, why should we be?"

Titus swore. "Because you're standing in my office, dripping melted snow all over my floor instead of being up in the mountains waiting for him."

"We're going to need snowmobiles," Butch said. "There's no way anyone is driving very far in the mountains right now. We'll find him. We're taking Lloyd with us. But what do you want us to do about the woman with him?" The banker gave him an impatient look. "We'll take care of all of it," Butch said quickly. "Don't we always?"

Titus could have argued further, but it would have been a waste of time. "Diamond thinks he can come into my town and make a fool out of me? I don't want him or his girlfriend coming out of those mountains. Is that understood? By spring there should be not enough left of his body to know how he died, right?"

Rafe nodded. "The animals will see to that."

"Make sure you dump the remains where some horn hunter doesn't stumble across them this spring."

"You got it," Butch said. "We'll let you know when it's done."

Titus shooed them out of his office and told his secretary to get maintenance to come up and clean up the mess the two had made. Then he sat back and looked out at the whirling snow again.

His father wasn't going to like this. Then again, Marcus didn't like the way he ran much about the business. It was time for Marcus to step down, but the old fool was healthy and stubborn and still thought he was running things.

"This kid was Charley Diamond's protégé. His legacy. Hell, practically his flesh-and-blood heir," Marcus Grandville had said on the call this morning. "So he outsmarted you last night and walked away with the poker money. Cut your losses. I'm warning you. We don't want him coming back to Butte. From what I've heard, he's in a position where he could do great harm to our business."

Titus still didn't believe that. Diamond was a cheap conman. But even if he did believe it, things had progressed such that it was too late. He had Keira Cross right where he wanted her and thus he had DJ. He couldn't tell his father that the reason he wanted DJ dead had little to do with the money lost last night or even the embarrassment of DJ getting the better of him. No, this went way back to when he was a kid. Humiliation was something that had stuck with him all these years—and DJ Diamond had witnessed it.

Now it was just a matter of finishing this. Then he would run the business as he saw fit. But he wondered if it would be possible as long as his father was alive.

"ARE YOU SURE I can't help?" Sadie asked as she heard DJ banging pots and pans in the tiny kitchen behind her. He'd told her to just take a seat in front of the fire, warm up and relax. He was going to cook.

"You cook?" she'd questioned.

"I can cook," he'd assured her. "But this will be more a case of opening canned goods.

"I've got everything under control," he called back now.

She stared into the flames, wondering how true that was. If what Lloyd had told him was true, Keira had set DJ up. Meeting her up here in the mountains seemed like a death wish. Was DJ really that sure he could trust this girl he'd called his little sister?

She thought about PI Buck Crawford. She didn't doubt that it was true, DJ had a twin sister. She knew there was more to the story. Hadn't the PI said that DJ and his twin's mother had thought both babies had died? That they'd later been given away? Sadie just hoped there was some good news to be had with his biological family. She wasn't sure how much more bad DJ could take—especially if Keira betrayed him.

"I hope you're hungry," he said from behind her, startling her out of her thoughts. She caught a whiff of something that smelled wonderful and felt her stomach rumble. "It's my own concoction. I hope you like it."

He handed her a bowl and spoon. "It's a can of spaghetti mixed with a can of chili. I added a few spices I found." He sounded so eager as he waited for her to take a bite.

She breathed in the rather unusual mixed scents, filled her spoon and took a bite. Surprisingly the canned spaghetti and the chili actually went together. "This is delicious."

"Don't sound so shocked," he joked.

She took another bite. "Seriously, it's really good."

He laughed, shaking his head before returning to the kitchen to load his own bowl. He joined her in front of the fire in the opposite chair. "You really like it?"

"I love it. I hadn't realized how hungry I was until I tasted it."

She could see that he was pleased as he began to eat his. They ate in a companionable silence. The only sound the occasional crackle of the fire. Outside, the snow continued to fall as if it were never going to stop. She could see flakes fly by the window, whirling through the pines outside. Sometimes she heard the soft moan of the wind. Outside there was only white. With a start she realized something. They were snowed in here. Trapped.

The thought startled her until she reminded herself that if they couldn't leave, then no one could get to them. The rental SUV was down the mountain, blocking the road. She couldn't help but wonder. Where was Keira?

As she finished her dinner, DJ offered her more, but she shook her head, pleasantly full. He took her spoon and bowl and went to finish off what he'd made. She found herself lulled by the crackling fire, the warmth, the fullness in her stomach.

It felt so pleasantly domestic that she could almost forget why they were here in this cabin and what they would be facing when the storm stopped. As she glanced over at DJ, she wanted to pretend that they had stumbled onto a magical cabin and they could stay here forever, safe from a dangerous outside world. In here, no one could hurt them.

Childish wishing, she thought. There were no magical cabins, no place safe from the dangerous out-

side world because of the life they both had lived—
and were still living. Was she kidding herself that
she could stop doing this? Just get off, like climbing
from a merry-go-round? Could DJ?

Otherwise, *they* were that dangerous world.

MARCUS GRANDVILLE KEPT going over his morning
conversation with his son. The fool had authorized
a poker game with DJ Diamond and two of Titus's
men. The PI Marcus had met got involved. DJ walked
away with the money after besting Titus's men.

"What kind of foolishness was this?" Marcus had
demanded. "I told you to settle and get him out of
town. What about that didn't you understand, Titus?"

"I couldn't just let this bastard come into town,
set up a poker game, take us to the cleaners and walk
away. One of your associates, Frank Burns, was in
the game. DJ was thumbing his nose at us."

"So what?"

"You're beginning to get soft in your old age if
you'd let a Diamond come into our town and do
whatever he damned well pleases."

"Oh, and you handled it so much better? DJ Diamond did exactly what he planned and now he's left
town after rubbing your face in it. Isn't that why
you're so upset? You thought you could outsmart
him and you failed."

"He hasn't gotten away," Titus said. "I have him
right where I want him. I have Keira Cross, the woman

he calls his little sister. I have her and therefore, I have Diamond."

"What are you talking about?"

"I'm using her to get DJ. I know exactly where he's headed and when he gets there, I'm going to make sure that he never comes back to Butte again."

Marcus shook his head, thinking now that he should have tried to talk his son out of this plan. Titus had always been a hothead. He didn't understand business, legit business; he never would. He wanted to be the tough guy, the schoolyard bully. He didn't even know how to pick his fights.

Now he'd sent Rafe, Butch and Lloyd into the mountains. Marcus knew what that meant. Titus wouldn't be happy until Diamond was dead. He swore under his breath as more of the conversation got under his skin.

"You used to let Charley run all over you. I'm not going to let DJ Diamond run roughshod over me."

Marcus shook his head. Titus could never understand the respect he and Charley Diamond had for each other. "I let him run his small-time cons in my town. Because I knew that he could never hurt me unless I did something stupid and tried to keep him from making a living here. You never learned how to make deals because you always have to win. You think I've gone soft? I'm washing my hands of this whole mess. You're on your own just like you've always wanted. If you're looking for my blessing, you're not getting it. You're making a huge mistake. Probably your last."

Now he regretted his words. He feared for his son. Worse for what this might do to the Grandville name—and their business. Titus was a fool, and he was about to prove it to the world.

DJ FINISHED EATING the rest of what he'd made, then cleaned up the dishes in the water he'd heated on the stove. He couldn't help smiling. He could see Charley in this cabin. It was comfortable and yet simple, like Charley himself. Why his uncle had never told him about the place still surprised him. Especially since Keira knew about it.

He pushed the thought away as he finished the dishes, dried them and put them away. Returning to the fire, he found Sadie sound asleep. He stared down at her, feeling a wave of affection for her that threatened to drop him to his knees. When had he fallen in love with her?

He felt blindsided. All that time when he'd been flirting and joking with her knowing she only saw him as an arrogant fool, she'd somehow sneaked into his heart and made a home there. She was right. He was a fool.

Leaning down, he kissed her forehead, then carefully, he picked her up and carried her the few feet to the double bed. He took off her boots and covered her with several of the extra quilts on a rack by the bed. She stirred a little but went right back to sleep.

It had been a long, exhausting day, after a long, uncomfortable night in the back of the SUV.

For a moment, he watched her sleep. She looked so peaceful, as if she didn't have a care in the world. He realized that he didn't know if she had a man in her life. He knew she lived in a penthouse condo next to the ocean, that she drove a nice car that she'd bought with money she'd earned herself, that she had Sunday dinner with her godfather each week and that she didn't like the mustache DJ had grown shortly after they'd first met. He'd shaved it off before the next time he saw her. But that's about all he knew about her.

Turning away, he went back to the fire. He was exhausted but knew he wouldn't be able to sleep. His heart ached for so many reasons. Now he felt as if he'd come to a crossroads in his life. He could keep looking back at the paths he'd taken or he could look to the future—a far different future than he had ever imagined.

Was it possible that he had a twin sister? Ansley Brookshire. A blood relative. And he had a mother who'd believed that both he and Ansley had died at birth. And family, half siblings.

For so long he'd wondered who he was and why no one had wanted him, thankful that Charley had taken him in when he had no one else. If true that Ansley was his twin, it brought up a lot of questions. Like what had happened to separate them? Where was their mother? Why hadn't someone come looking for him sooner?

He realized he wasn't all that sure he wanted to know the answers. Maybe it would be better not to know the truth.

He glanced over at Sadie sleeping on the bed. Partners. More than partners. Did she feel the same way about him that he felt about her?

His beating heart assured him she had to. Why else was she here risking her life to help him?

He thought about Keira and questioned why he had to know the truth. Why he had to face her. He would be facing his past. If she'd betrayed him, then nothing had been as he'd thought.

Once the storm stopped, he would know the truth. If Keira had betrayed him, she might not even come to the cabin. Instead the Grandvilles' thugs, Butch Lamar and Rafe Westfall, would. He told himself that right now they would have the same problem he did, so he didn't expect them until the storm blew through. According to the weatherman the last they'd heard on the radio, the storm wasn't supposed to let up until the day after tomorrow.

So they had time, he told himself. He had time to decide what to do.

He'd always had a different idea about what made up family. Not blood. Not love. Not even loyalty. Family had been Charley and Keira. At best, he'd hoped they would have his back. Now, he feared both would have sold him out to save their own skins. And that could be exactly what Keira had done.

Either way, he couldn't worry about it now, he thought as he rose and stepped out on the porch. He listened as the snow blew past. Absolute silence. No sound of a vehicle. Nothing but the whisper of wind blowing the falling snow. He could feel the temperature dropping as he went around the side of the cabin to get more firewood. It would be a long night.

He was just glad he'd found this cabin. He didn't think they would have survived in the pickup even with the engine running and the heater going. They would have run out of gas, run out of hope, fairly soon. He told himself he could relax a little as he went back inside. Sadie was safe.

Now all he had to do was keep her that way.

Chapter Fourteen

Buck had been sure he could beat DJ and Sadie up to the cabin. He and the Colts had the shorter drive if they were anywhere around Butte, but DJ had also gotten a head start. But as they had just started up in the mountains a tire blew on the snowmobile trailer. They had to take the machines off to fix it. They'd lost any chance they had at getting to the cabin before DJ, and now it was getting dark.

The conditions had been worse than even he and Tommy and James had thought they would be—especially in the dark, but no one suggested turning back. It became apparent quickly that once they reached the mountains, they wouldn't make it all the way to Charley's cabin.

"Don't Francis and Bob Reiner have a cabin up here?" James had asked.

Buck tried to calculate where they were. "Not far ahead." His pickup was bucking snowdrifts. It wouldn't be that long before they couldn't go any farther by truck. They'd have to take the snowmo-

biles, but not in this storm in the dark. In his headlights, he could barely make out the narrow road
through the pines.

"Watch for the sign," he said. "We can spend the
night there and try again in the morning. DJ is going
to be having the same problem on the other side."

They'd gone a few miles when Tommy said,
"There's the sign."

Buck turned and drove up the road toward the
cabin, but he didn't get far before the truck high-
centered on a huge drift. The wind whipped snow
around them as he shut off the engine.

"That's as far as we're going," he said, afraid this
had been a mistake. He hadn't been surprised when
James and Tommy had insisted on coming along.
Sheriff Willie Colt was standing by, offering a helicopter when the storm stopped, if needed. So far
no crime had been committed. Buck was hoping to
end this without gunplay, but that would depend on
what they found up here on this mountain.

They grabbed their gear and started up through
the whirling snow, breaking through drifts, until
they reached the front door of the cabin. The Rein-
ers never locked the front door, saying they'd rather
not have anyone break in. They didn't keep guns or
liquor, and nothing worth carting out of the mountains to pawn. They'd never had a break-in or anything stolen.

James opened the door as Buck grabbed a load
of firewood from the overhang on the porch. Within
minutes they had a fire going in the woodstove.

"I can tell you're having second thoughts," James said after they'd eaten one of the sandwiches Lori had sent.

"I should have come alone," Buck said.

"Wasn't going to happen, so get over it. If you feel really bad, you can take one of the kid bunk beds. I'm going for the double bed in the only adult-sized bedroom," James said with a grin. "Looks like Tommy has already taken the couch." Tommy was sprawled out trying to get a bar on his phone.

"You can take the truck back in the morning," Buck told him.

"I'm not worried about Bella," Tommy denied. "Baby's not due for a month and you know Bella, she wouldn't want me worrying. Just wanted to check in, that's all." Buck and James exchanged a look.

"Just in case you are worried in the morning, take the truck. Charley's cabin isn't that far by snowmobile. I am wondering if Keira Diamond Cross didn't get us all up here on a fool's errand while she's on her way to Alaska."

"That could be the best scenario," James said.

"Maybe for her. That still leaves DJ to deal with the Grandvilles if I'm right and this woman he calls his little sister set him up."

"I guess we'll find out tomorrow," James said, and yawned. "Try to get some sleep. Tomorrow could be a busy, eventful day."

SADIE WOKE TO the smell of something frying. She opened her eyes to see DJ at the small stove. It felt too early to wake up and yet there was DJ with a pancake turner in his hand humming softly as he cooked whatever was sizzling in that huge cast-iron skillet.

Next to the bed, she could see that there was fresh wood on the fire. How long had he been up? Or had he ever come to bed? She tried to remember going to bed and couldn't.

Had DJ put her under the covers last night? She threw back the heavy quilts covering her, not surprised to see that she was fully clothed. DJ wouldn't have taken advantage of her exhaustion. No, he had a code of honor that he followed. The thought touched her, warming her heart.

If he wanted to bed her, he'd seduce her. The thought made her swallow as she saw her boots were positioned next to each other beside the bed and slipped them on.

"Is that breakfast I smell?" she said, walking the few yards into the kitchen. It was still storming outside. She couldn't see anything but snow through the windows, as if the cabin had been wrapped in cotton.

"Hey, sleeping beauty. I wondered if you planned to sleep all day." He was grinning, those blue eyes of his bright in the white light coming through the windows. Looking at him, it was as if he didn't have a care in the world except what to cook next. She could see that he felt at home here as basic as the place was. That, too, made her smile.

"What is that?" she asked, taking in what was frying in the skillet.

"Are you telling me that you've never had Spam?"

"I've never heard of it," she said skeptically.

"Well, then you are in for a treat."

He was giving her the hard sell, which was making her even more skeptical. *"You made flour tortillas?"* This man continued to amaze her.

His grin broadened. "I found flour in an airtight canister and canned shortening and salt. Voilà! Flour tortillas and Spam and canned salsa. This morning, we feast. Shall I make you a Diamond burrito?"

She nodded, laughing as she did. "I'm guessing this isn't your first time eating canned meat."

His grin faded a little as he shook his head. "We could sit at the kitchen table," he suggested, nodding toward a folding table and chairs that he'd set up near the front door.

She hadn't noticed. But she did notice that it looked like fresh blood on his shirtsleeve. "Right after breakfast, I need to re-bandage your arm." He started to argue but she talked over him. "I'm sure I can find something to use here in the cabin."

"There's a first aid kit in the top drawer over there," he said, nodding in the direction of the cabinets along the wall to the back door. She marveled at how he'd made himself at home. It made her wonder about the man he called Uncle Charley. Apparently they had a lot in common.

BUCK AWOKE IN the middle of the night to snow. He'd hoped that the storm would have stopped. It hadn't. He heard Tommy and James moving somewhere in the cabin. He tried his cell phone. No service. According to his calculations, they still had a way to go before they reached Charley Diamond's cabin. He had no idea if DJ and Sadie had made it there. Or what they had found if they had. His stomach churned at the thought that he might be too late.

James had been subdued last night. Tommy seemed restless. Was he worried about Bella? Bringing them along had been a mistake, Buck told himself, then was reminded how much trouble he would have had changing that tire last night in the storm if he'd been alone.

"You two okay?" he asked as they began to put on their warm clothes to leave.

"Let's do this," James said, and looked at his brother. Tommy nodded.

"It's only a half mile up the road before the turn to the cabin. I doubt we'll get that far before we have to unload the snowmobiles and go the rest of the way on them. With luck, DJ and Sadie are still okay."

Both looked solemn as he glanced outside. All he could see was white. Out of the corner of his eye, he saw James check his weapon. Tommy did the same. Buck had already made sure his was loaded, even though he didn't want any gunplay.

But he'd heard stories about the Grandvilles and the men who worked for the family. DJ had already been shot. Guns were a part of this world—and the one Buck now considered his new career as a PI. Most private investigators, though, didn't even carry guns. Few had ever been forced to use them.

Unfortunately, Buck feared today would not be one of those days.

That's when he heard the buzz of snowmobiles. More than one. All headed their way.

DJ HANDED SADIE a plate with her burrito on it. "I gave you extra salsa. I know how you love your hot peppers." His grin was back and she tried to relax, telling herself that they wouldn't be up here in the mountains all that long. Once they reached civilization again, she'd insist he have his wound checked out. She worried it would get infected. Better to worry about a flesh wound than what might happen before they got off this mountain.

If she had to, she'd call her godfather. He'd know someone who knew someone who knew someone who would check out the gunshot wound and not report it. Not that she wanted her godfather to know where she was and why. He wouldn't like it, that much she knew.

"Keep it professional," he'd warned her. "DJ Diamond will make a great partner for what I have him doing, but beyond that…" He shook his head. "He's not boyfriend material, so don't get too attached."

At that time, she hadn't met DJ yet and had rolled her eyes. "You don't have to worry. I won't touch him with a ten-foot pole."

Her godfather, who had already met DJ, had said, "Keep it that way. I've been told he has an irresistible charm that's like catnip for women. I hear you're falling for his routine, and I'll put someone else with him."

She'd been fine with that at the time. Now she knew that no one could have done the job she and DJ had for her godfather. Her godfather knew it, too. He'd just assumed now that DJ had paid off his uncle Charley's debt that his goddaughter wouldn't be seeing the young Diamond again. She'd let her godfather believe that because she'd thought it was probably true. Once she told DJ that his bill was paid in full, he'd be gone.

Sadie hadn't admitted to herself, let alone DJ or her godfather, that it was the last thing she wanted. She had more than a soft spot for the cowboy.

"Well?" DJ asked. When she didn't immediately respond, he glanced at her plate and the half-eaten burrito on it. She hadn't even realized that she'd taken a bite. Half of it was already gone.

"Delicious. Sorry, I was just enjoying it. Do you need me to tell you that you're a great cook?"

He was eyeing her as if he'd seen that her mind had been miles away. "Great, huh?"

"Great," she said and ducked her head to take another bite. "I'm a Spam fan now."

"Good to hear, since we might be eating a lot of it, depending on when this storm lets up. But I hope you know that I can see through any lie that comes out of that mouth of yours," he said quietly, his gaze on her mouth.

She swallowed the bite of burrito, her cheeks heating under the directness of his look.

Sadie heard it about the same time as DJ did. He set down his plate and was on his feet in an instant. By the time he reached the front window, she was beside him. "Someone's coming, aren't they?"

"Stay here." He pulled on his coat, one of the weapons in his hand as he went out the front door, closing it behind him, before he stepped off the porch and disappeared into the falling snow.

DJ DIDN'T GO FAR before he stopped to listen. He could hear the whine of the snowmobiles somewhere on the mountain. It didn't sound close, but it was hard to tell.

Who was it? Keira? Or someone else foolish enough to try to get to their cabin in this storm? Someone like Butch Lamar and Rafe Westfall? Not Titus. He didn't do his own dirty work.

It had sounded as if the machines were busting through snowdrifts. He waited for the buzz to get louder, signifying that they were headed this way. But that didn't happen. The sound died off. They weren't headed here. At least not yet, he thought as he went to the woodpile.

But now he was on alert. It had felt as if they were alone on the mountain. Just the two of them. And he'd liked it. Liked it a lot more than he'd wanted to admit. Now he feared they didn't have that much more time together.

Sadie looked up expectantly when he came through the door. She'd taken their plates to the sink and was washing them. But next to her on the counter was her gun, fully loaded, he knew.

"Whoever it was didn't come this way." He was relieved. He wanted this time before seeing Keira. He realized that he also wanted this time with Sadie.

"You think they were looking for us?" she asked.

"Didn't sound like it. Our tracks would have been covered and they wouldn't have been able to see the SUV up here hidden in the pines and snow. As long as it's snowing, I doubt they'd be able to see the smoke from our fire." Unless they stopped, got out and smelled it.

He saw her visibly relax as he took off his boots and coat and hung them up, his gun tucked in the back of his jeans. The other gun he'd taken from Rafe and Butch was on the mantel behind a large wooden vase. Both were loaded if needed. He hoped it wouldn't come to that, but then again he couldn't imagine any other way out of this. If the Grandvilles' thugs showed up, then Keira had to be in on the setup—even if she didn't show herself.

"Thanks for breakfast," Sadie said, drying her hands on a paper towel. "Where did you say I could find that first aid kit?"

"First, I brought you something."

She frowned quizzically. "At the local convenience store you stopped at on your way back in the cabin?"

"Something like that. It's right outside the door on the porch."

Sadie was still giving him a questioning look as

she stepped to the door, opened and saw a small evergreen tree leaning against the side of the cabin.

"I thought it was small enough that we could find something to decorate it with around the cabin."

She turned to stare at him. "A real Christmas tree."

He shrugged. "You said you never had one. I found an axe near the woodpile and since it is the season…"

Tears welled in her eyes, and he felt his heart ache. It had been impulsive and such a small thing to him, but so much more to her. "DJ."

He heard so much in those two letters. He cleared his throat. "I'll make a stand for it."

"Thank you."

He could only shrug again, half afraid of what he'd say—let alone do—seeing the emotion in her eyes.

HE'D CUT HER a Christmas tree. Sadie feared she would cry if she tried to speak so she could only nod as she closed the door. His thoughtfulness was almost her undoing. She went back to the fire, warmed her hands and steadied herself before she asked, "Where did you say that first aid kit was?"

She was surprised to find that her hands were trembling as she opened the box with the red cross on it. DJ had taken off his shirt. She'd seen him without one enough times, but seeing him half-naked in the close confines of the small cabin made it much more intimate.

Sadie tried to concentrate as she took off the old makeshift bandage. She could feel DJ watching her closely. She cleaned and gently put antiseptic on the wound before she re-bandaged it. Closing the first aid kit, she started to stand to return it to the cabinet when DJ laid a hand on her arm.

She froze as his touch sent a bolt of electricity charging through her at the speed of lightning before it settled in her center. She tried to breathe but it made her chest hurt.

"Sadie." He'd never said her name like that. Low, husky, loaded with a jolt of emotion that she recognized even though she'd never felt it with such intensity.

She slowly raised her gaze to his. What she saw in those unusually pale blue eyes made her heart kick-start. She let out the breath. She hadn't realized that she'd still been holding the first aid kit as DJ took it from her and set it aside.

Her mouth went dry as he locked eyes with her. She tried to swallow as he rose and gently pulled her closer. She wanted to drag her gaze from his. She wanted to pull away, but all the reasons this was a bad idea evaded her. She wanted this, and from the look in his eyes, he wanted it just as desperately.

Drawing her closer, he bent to tenderly kiss her. Her lips parted of their own accord and she heard a soft moan escape him. He dragged her to him, the look in his eyes telegraphing the message *Stop. Me. At. Any. Time.*

But stopping him was the last thing she wanted.

He pulled her against him, her soft to his hard, and then they were kissing like lovers. His hands slid down her back to her behind. He cupped her, pulling her against him. She heard his moan.

He drew back to look at her. She could see he was begging her to stop him. He didn't want to hurt her. He didn't want her to just be another of the women he'd bedded and walked away from.

"If you stop now, I will never forgive you," she said, her voice breaking.

He shook his head. "You have no idea how long I have wanted this. Wanted you."

"So what's stopping you?"

He chuckled. "Your godfather will kill me. But he'll have to wait in line." He swept her up into his arms and carried her over to the bed. The moment he set her down, she pulled him down with her. The kiss was all heat. Their tongues met, teased, then took. They tore at each other's clothes in reckless abandonment.

There was no turning back as he bent over her breasts, sucking, nipping, teasing with his tongue. Outside the wind howled at the eaves, the snow fell as if never going to stop, and inside DJ made love to her as if there might not be a tomorrow. Later, after they were curled together trying to catch their breaths, he whispered next to her, "You intrigued me from the first time I laid eyes on you. Then I got to know you."

She chuckled as she turned to him. "I could take that a number of ways."

"You were pretty and smart and sexy as all get-out. Sitting across from you all those nights, I wanted you, but I also wanted more than anything I'd ever had with another woman." His gaze met hers and held. "When you got off that plane the other day...I knew. I love you, Sadie Montclair."

"You don't have to say that."

"I've never said it to another woman—even at gunpoint. I wasn't sure how much longer I could work with you and not...step over a line that would end it."

She'd never seen him this serious. "DJ," she whispered as she moved to kiss him.

He looked uncomfortable, as if he'd opened his heart, laid it out in front of her and now felt too vulnerable. "If I'd just known that all it would take was a misshapen little evergreen tree to get you into bed..." he joked.

Sadie knew this man so well. "I didn't sleep with you because you brought me a Christmas tree. I've wanted this for a very long time too." She smiled and said, "I fell in love with you as hard as I tried not to. I love you, DJ. Do I need to tell you that's the first time I've said those words to a man?"

He shook his head. "So it wasn't my imagination? This has been building for some time?" She nodded.

"I never thought..." He didn't have to finish. She knew what he was saying. He never thought the two of them would ever be together like this. "I did think about you and me, though. But I saw us in a fancy hotel with silken sheets and room service. Nor did

I ever think it could be so amazing, not even in my wildest dreams." He traced a finger along her cheek to her lips.

She smiled. Her gaze locked with his. "The room service here is quite good and I don't need expensive sheets with a high thread count. Just being here with you like this…" She touched the washboard of his stomach. "I feel I'm never going to get enough of you."

He laughed as he grabbed her and rolled her over so she was flat on the bed and he leaned above her. "Let me see what I can do about that." He bent down to kiss her gently on the lips before he trailed kisses down her neck. She closed her eyes, remembering that his favorite song was something about a slow hand.

Chapter Fifteen

When DJ woke beside Sadie, he was afraid that earlier had been nothing more than a dream. In the corner was the small Christmas tree they'd taken a break from lovemaking to decorate together with the silly things they'd found in the cabin. It made him smile it was so ugly and yet so beautiful all at the same time. Then they'd gone back to bed to make love and had fallen asleep.

He glanced over at Sadie and wanted to pinch himself. He'd never thought he'd even get to kiss her. The woman had captivated him for so long, but it had been strictly hands-off, all business. He ran his gaze down the length of her naked body, memorizing it the way he had earlier with his fingertips, with his tongue, with his lips—as if he could ever forget.

Remembering made his heart beat faster. He'd never experienced this kind of pleasure and pain, and knew it was why he'd never put his heart in jeopardy before. The emotions he was experiencing were the most joyous he'd ever known—and the most terrifying. Yet his pulse drummed with more than desire as he realized he couldn't bear to ever walk away from this woman. He felt as if he would die with the longing. As if he wouldn't be able to breathe—and wouldn't care if he did.

He'd never felt anything like this, and it scared him more than having killers after them. This woman had stolen not just his heart, but his body and soul. He'd always felt protective of her, but now—

Her brown eyes opened, her gaze on his face as if she'd felt him looking at her. He smiled, not in the least embarrassed to be caught. "I'll never get tired of looking at you."

He saw the heat in her eyes as she reached for him, but just as quickly, she froze. Her gaze shot over his shoulder to the front of the house. He felt himself tense and quickly estimated how long it would take him to get to the weapon behind the vase on the mantel.

"It stopped snowing," she said in a whisper filled with regret.

He felt it, too. Being here like this, he'd forgotten the outside world for a while. Now it came rushing back in. With the storm stopped, someone could get to them. He felt both dread and regret. "We'd better get up."

She nodded but didn't let go of his forearm. Looking into her eyes, he knew she was afraid this might be their last time together. He bent toward her for a kiss, and she cupped the back of his head, drawing him closer.

He wanted this so badly, and not just for today but always. He knew he would do whatever it took to make sure that happened as he lost himself in her. One way or another, they would be together. Partners to the end, he thought.

BY THE TIME they were out of bed and dressed, the sun had come out. The sunshine lit up the freshly fallen snow. It glittered like diamonds, so bright that it was blinding. Even the pine needles under the cover of snow caught the rays and glistened.

"It's so beautiful," Sadie said from the window. "Like a field of diamonds." She turned as DJ came in through the back door, reminding herself how dangerous it could be.

"I found a shovel in the shed behind the cabin," DJ said. "I'm going to dig out the SUV and then we're getting out of here."

She stared at him in surprise. "What about Keira?"

He shook his head. "Hopefully she's on her way to Alaska."

"Are you sure about this?" She couldn't bear the thought that he'd have regrets. That their lovemaking had been the cause of him wanting to leave.

DJ's look was heartbreaking. "I don't need to look her in the eye to know the answer. I just didn't want to believe it." He shrugged. "At some point, you have to quit trying to save a person."

She wasn't sure he was still talking about Keira. She quickly stepped to him and put a finger to his lips. She shook her head slowly until his gaze met hers and held. She kissed him, wanting desperately to be in his arms, to assure him that she wasn't ever going to give up on him. But even as she had those thoughts, she realized how much she needed this man.

She'd always been independent, determinedly so. While her godfather had raised her and made sure she had anything she wanted, she'd been on her own since she was eighteen. She could take care of herself, something she prided herself on. She'd never needed a man to take care of her.

Nor had she ever wanted one badly enough to even consider giving up her independence, let alone admitting that need. Until DJ Diamond. Neither of them had relationships that had lasted. The two of them as partners had been the longest for both of them.

Her need for DJ filled her with panic that she might lose him. They'd finally admitted how they felt about each other. She'd kept it bottled up for so long. It was unbearable even letting him go down to get the SUV unstuck. That need was an excruciating ache, so physically painful that she wanted to beg him not to leave for fear of what would happen.

But as she met his eyes, she saw that they couldn't stay up here on this mountain forever. Eventually they would have to leave and go back to the real world. If their love for each other couldn't withstand that, then there was no future for them.

She stepped back, feeling bereft. Love hurts. The words from a song now resonated in her heart, in the pounding of her blood.

"That vehicle we heard before," she asked. "Keira?"

He shrugged. "Could have been Grandville's men. Could have been anyone."

She knew it could also be PI Buck Crawford—with more of the PIs from Colt Brothers Investigation. Crawford was determined to get DJ to his twin's wedding. She could only hope that was the case and that DJ made it. He had family waiting for him.

Buck woke to the sound of the snowmobiles. He sat up, banged his head on the upper bunk and swore. What time was it?

Climbing out of the bed, he hurriedly pulled on his boots since he'd slept in his clothes in the cold cabin.

Before he got his second boot on, James opened the door. "You hear that?"

He nodded. "Sounds like more than one."

"Sounds like they're headed our way."

"Willie?"

James shook his head. "The sheriff's department doesn't move that quickly, especially in a snowstorm. You think it's DJ?"

"I doubt he had access to a trailer and snowmobiles. Grandville's men."

"That's what I'm afraid of," Tommy said from the

doorway. "They must have seen your truck and the snowmobile trailer outside the cabin. Sounds like there are three of them coming up the mountain. What do you want to do?"

"They aren't looking for us, right?" James asked.

"Guess we'll have to find out." Buck pulled on his second boot and rose.

By the time they reached the cabin's front door, all three snowmobiles and their drivers were sitting outside. Buck opened the door and stepped out, James and Tommy following.

"Where's DJ Diamond?"

"Who wants to know?" Buck asked over the rumble of the three snowmobile engines.

"Butch, it's that PI I told you about." Buck recognized the man's voice who'd spoken. Lloyd from the poker party. He seemed nervous, his hand on the weapon at his side.

But it was Butch Lamar he kept his eye on. He'd met other men like Butch. Grandville's lead thug was a big man, with a face that had met too many other men's fists and an unfriendly attitude. They were always looking for a fight. They liked beating people up. They constantly were looking for someone to knock that chip off their shoulder. Butch Lamar was one of them.

Buck assumed the third man was Rafe Westfall. Both Butch and Rafe had AKs hanging across their chests and pistols at their hips over their winter clothing.

"We have business with Diamond," Butch said.

He knew what kind of business. "So do we. Also we have the sheriff on his way just in case your business includes hurting Diamond or the woman with him," Buck said.

Butch wagged his head as if amused. "I don't think you know who you're dealing with."

"Trust me, I do," Buck said.

"And where's this law? I don't see any law. Rafe, do you see any law?" He turned back to Buck. "From the looks of it, we have the upper hand here. He touched the AK-47 strapped to his chest. This is a dangerous place to be for you boys. Anything can happen up here this time of year. A man could get himself killed really easy."

Butch's words hung in the air. An open challenge.

James saw Lloyd go for his pistol before Buck did. He drew his weapon from behind him and fired at the same time Lloyd did. Buck was drawing his gun as well when Butch gunned his snowmobile, the others following suit as they sped off, Lloyd hunched over his machine in pain, the snow where he'd been sitting on his machine dotted red with blood.

Buck turned quickly to James, who was holding his side. He looked at Tommy who hadn't had a chance to go for his gun. He was thankful since it could have been worse if they had pulled their weapons. "Get inside. Let's see how bad you're hit."

"Not bad," James said as he was helped inside the cabin to a chair.

"I'll be the judge of that," Buck said. "Tommy, disconnect the snowmobile trailer from the truck."

"Aren't we going after them?"

"No, you're taking James down the mountain so Willie can get a helicopter to take him to the hospital."

As soon as Tommy went outside, Buck looked to see how badly James had been hit. There was a lot of blood. He did what he could to stop the bleeding and prepare the wound for traveling. "Keep this on the wound," he said of the gauze and bandage he'd found in the bathroom cabinet.

"I know what you're thinking," James said. "But you can't go after those three alone."

"You need to get to the hospital," Buck said. "Tommy needs to take you. Once you're where you can use your phone, get Willie to send up deputies and Feds. Don't worry about me. I'll be fine," Buck said.

James shook his head as Tommy came back in. "The truck's ready. How's James?"

"He needs to get to the hospital. You're taking him," Buck said, expecting more argument. But one look at how pale James had gone and Tommy nodded. "He's lost a lot of blood. I did what I could. Get him off this mountain."

James grabbed Buck's arm. "I'm planning to stand up with you at your wedding, man. Don't let me down."

Buck smiled. "I'll be there. Now go. They might decide to circle back. I want them to think we all left. Tommy, drive the truck down following their tracks to their vehicle. They would have busted through the drifts. It should make the going easier."

"You do realize that we are going to have to disable their vehicle, right?" James said.

"You need medical attention. Tommy, don't listen to him. Just get him to the hospital. Tell the sheriff hello."

"Willie will be coming like gangbusters," Tommy said. "Just keep yourself safe until he and the troops arrive."

ANSLEY HAD BEEN waiting anxiously by the phone. She'd wrapped the rest of the Christmas presents she'd purchased and put them around the tree. She'd cleaned the kitchen, made a batch of cookies and was just about to ice them when her phone finally rang.

Hurriedly, she scooped up her cell. "Buck?"

"Sorry, it's me," Bella said. "I'm in labor."

It was the last thing she'd expected to hear.

"Don't panic," her friend said quickly. "I called my doctor. He said not to come in until my contractions were more consistent and much closer together. I've called Lori. She just put the twins down for a nap. She assured me that I might not be having this baby for hours—or maybe not even today. She called Ellie while I called Carla. Ellie's in Seattle at her law firm. Carla didn't pick up."

"I'll be right there," Ansley said, knowing that Bella had to be wishing she'd reached someone with at least pregnancy experience. She checked to make sure that the stove was off. The cookies could wait. "I'm leaving now."

Bella laughed. "I know I'm being silly, but this is all new and I'm nervous."

"I am a great hand-holder," Ansley assured her. "Have you been able to reach Tommy?"

"No, that's the other thing. I haven't heard a word since they went up into the mountains yesterday. I know he doesn't want to miss this. He better not miss this." Her voice broke.

"I'm sure he'll be back before you even have to go to the hospital," she said, not sure of that at all. She knew nothing about giving birth or babies. But after she and Buck were married, she couldn't wait to learn. "Sit tight. I'll be there before you know it."

The moment she disconnected, she tried Buck's number. It went straight to voice mail. "Hey, it's me. Bella's in labor. Hope you're all right. Come back. Bella needs us all. I need you. I should never have sent you on this ridiculous mission." She hung up close to tears. Maribelle was right. She was a spoiled rich girl. Even as she thought it, she knew that wanting to have her twin at her wedding wasn't outrageous. It was her deepest desire. Unless, of course, her twin was a possible, even probable, criminal on the run and this ended up getting the people she loved killed.

DJ TOOK THE shovel down the mountain to the snowbound SUV and began digging. He needed the physical exertion. He went to work, shoveling as his mind raced. He kept thinking about Keira. Had he really been ready to jeopardize everything just to know whether or not she had betrayed him?

His thoughts rushed back to Sadie and the time they'd spent in the cabin. He didn't want to leave here for fear the bubble would pop. He'd told her that he loved her, but he wasn't sure that was enough. She'd said she loved him, too. But what would happen when they got back to the real world? If they got back?

He stopped to listen, hearing snowmobiles but far off in the distance; he glanced back up the mountain. He knew Sadie had taken the SUV keys the moment he couldn't find them. She didn't trust him and with good reason. He would do anything to protect her, even leave her behind if it came to that. But right now, he wasn't sure that Keira wouldn't show up. The cabin was no longer safe since the storm had passed. Keira might not be the only one coming for them.

Going back to his shoveling, he thought about Ansley Brookshire, his alleged twin sister, who was going to all this trouble so he'd be at her wedding. She really could be his twin, he thought with a chuckle. She was determined enough and they did look like they could be fraternal twins.

But how would she feel when she met him? She was a Brookshire. The name meant money. He was willing to bet that her childhood had been nothing like his own. She probably didn't realize who she might be inviting not only to her wedding but also into her life.

He tried to imagine being part of this family Crawford had told him about. He would have been a complete fool not to realize that this was the fork in the road, the crossroads he'd felt coming. His deal with Sadie and her godfather had come to an end, but that didn't mean that he and Sadie couldn't have a future. A twin sister was offering him a family. And then there was Keira, who was either going to Alaska to live with her no-account husband or setting him up for a fall.

DJ stopped shoveling. With luck, he should be able to drive the SUV out now. He leaned on the shovel as he tried to catch his breath. He'd made a decision about his future. He and Sadie were leaving.

Glancing back up the mountain, he smiled to himself. It was a no-brainer. Let go of the past, let Keira go to Alaska, leave the poker game money for the Grandvilles and walk away. One call to Marcus Grandville once they got off this mountain could end this.

He took a deep breath of the cold mountain air. It was almost Christmas. He thought of their Christmas tree back in the cabin. He was ready to experience the magic of the holiday through Sadie's eyes.

At the whine of a single snowmobile high on the mountain, he dropped the shovel. Whoever it was, they were headed this way and fast. Sadie. He had to get to her. He took off through the deep snow as he raced up the mountain, knowing that he would never reach the cabin before the snowmobile did.

Chapter Sixteen

Sadie had felt a chill as she stood on the porch and
looked down the mountainside to where she had
seen DJ shoveling. The breeze dislodged the fresh
snow from the pines, sending it streaming through
the sunlight, making the flakes gleam like glitter.
The mountainside was so quiet it was eerie. DJ had
said that they were leaving. He wasn't going to wait
for Keira. He wasn't going to leave her, either. She
had the keys to the SUV in her pocket, so she knew
he'd be back. But if she hadn't taken the keys, would
he have left?

If so it would have been to find his sister. He still
wanted the truth, she knew that. No matter what he
said, he had to know if Keira had betrayed him, set
him up to die. Sadie shuddered at the thought. How
could anyone want to hurt DJ? Once you looked into
his heart and saw what was there, it seemed impos-
sible.

She thought of their lovemaking. He'd been so
gentle with her, as if he was afraid she would break.

Yet she'd sensed the urgency in him. He'd wanted her for a long time. The man had amazing control, she thought with a wry smile. All the time they'd worked together, he'd joked, but he'd never let it go past that.

Sadie wouldn't have known how he felt if she hadn't seen it in his eyes. She'd thought she'd caught glimpses of it over their time together, but she'd never trusted it until now. DJ had said he loved her, something he'd never told another woman, and she believed him. Their lovemaking had been more than sex. There was a connection between them that felt so strong. The thought of losing it, losing DJ, made her stomach roil. They needed to get out of here, she thought urgently.

She hugged herself, shaken by that sudden almost warning. A part of her never wanted to leave this cabin, never wanted to go back into that world where things were complicated. Here, life was simple. But she knew they couldn't stay for so many reasons; Keira and Grandville's men were only part of it. DJ would never be happy with a life like this.

That was the problem, she thought, as she watched the breeze send the new snow into the cold morning air. She wasn't sure what it would take to make DJ happy. She wasn't sure he even knew himself. Could she make him happy once they left here?

Sadie just knew that it was important for him to make it back for his twin sister's wedding. She had no doubt after looking at Ansley's photo that it was true. He was the missing twin. He was born into a family that would love him. They'd gone to a lot of trouble to find him. It appeared to be the kind of family neither of them had ever had.

She silently urged DJ to hurry and get the SUV unstuck. The woods seemed too quiet. She felt a chill as she thought of Keira. Where was she? Had this been a trap? Sadie couldn't imagine what was in the woman's heart to do such a thing to DJ. She'd been glad to hear DJ say he wasn't staying around to wait for her. If not for the storm, she feared they would already know Keira's true intentions.

After everything that had happened between her and DJ since she met him, she would risk her life for his. She might have to let him go once they got off this mountain, but she couldn't live without knowing he was alive somewhere. She wanted to be able to think about him and imagine him in his Stetson sitting at a poker table. He'd be grinning, holding the winning cards in his hand because he was the best player at that table, and nothing was going to keep him from proving it.

Sadie heard the sound of a snowmobile. At first it was distant, but it was coming this way and fast. Her heart lurched. She looked down the mountain and didn't see DJ. He must have heard it, too.

She hurriedly stepped back inside the cabin and started for the mantel and the gun there when she heard the snowmobile engine stop. The silence was deafening. Until the back door of the cabin flew open, and she reached for the gun.

Ansley found Bella pacing the floor, her hand on her swollen abdomen, looking close to tears. "It's going to be fine," she assured her the moment she walked into the large ranch lodge. "I called Buck and left a message. I know they will turn back the moment they get it."

Bella didn't look any more convinced than Ansley. Who knew when they would get the message? Or if they would, since there was spotty cell service at best in the mountains and with this storm…

"Did you hear the avalanche report on the radio this morning?" Bella asked, sounding scared. "They're warning people to stay out of the mountains. The new snow on the old is too unstable. They said it is like a powder keg about to go off."

"Let's sit down," Ansley said. She'd heard the report. Like Bella, she was worried, but she couldn't show it. Bella was already upset enough. It couldn't be good for the baby. "I'm sure the men know what they're doing."

She didn't know the mountains around here, but she'd skied at both Bridger Bowl and Big Sky. There, though, the ski patrol cleared the cornices before letting skiers on the slopes. Cornices formed high in the mountains could be kicked off by anything— even a sound.

"I hope you're right," Bella said. "All this fresh snow, it just makes me so nervous."

Ansley felt the same way. Every year backcountry skiers and snowmobilers were caught in avalanches, many of them not surviving. Once the snow began to shift… The mountains would be extremely dangerous right now and Tommy, James and Buck had all gone up there.

"How far apart are your contractions?" She led Bella over to the living room couch, anxious to change the subject.

"They're sporadic," she said with a sigh. "But this girl is kicking like crazy. She is ready to come out of there."

"Why don't you put your feet up?" Ansley suggested. "Relax as much as you can. Your Christmas tree is beautiful. Tell me you didn't climb up on a ladder to decorate it yourself."

Bella rolled her eyes, seeing what she was trying to do. Still, Bella explained that Tommy had insisted she hire a crew to decorate the house. "He didn't want me overdoing it. Now I'm afraid maybe I did anyway and that's why the baby is coming early." She was clearly fighting tears.

"You don't know that," Ansley said, getting her some tissues. "We aren't even sure the baby is coming today." They sat in silence for a few minutes. "I feel like this is all my fault. If I hadn't been so determined to have my twin at my wedding…"

"Don't be silly," her friend said, sniffling as she wiped her eyes. "It's your determination that got you to us. None of this is your fault. We all just want your wedding to be perfect. Buck won't let you down, trust me. Anyway, this is what our men do. We wouldn't love them so much if they weren't the way they are."

Ansley nodded, knowing it was true. Buck was as driven as the Colt brothers in righting wrongs, helping people, finding out the truth. She loved that about him. All of them had helped her find her family and now they were doing their best to help the man Buck was convinced was her twin.

"So who do you think this woman is with DJ?" Bella asked.

"Sadie Montclair? I'm not even sure Buck knows. But he says there's something between them."

"Romantically?" Bella's eyes lit, making Ansley laugh.

"You are such a sucker for a happy ending," she teased. "I heard Davy is manning the office. I'll call him and see if he knows anything about her."

As she gave Davy what few details she knew about Sadie Montclair, Bella had another contraction. Ansley had been timing them, knowing that she might have to take her to the hospital soon. "Davy's going to call back."

They talked about baby names, baby clothes— "Have you seen the little overalls they make for girls?" Bella had cried. "I couldn't resist. I got the denim ones and the Western shirts that match."

"For a newborn?" Ansley asked in surprise.

"No, that would be silly. I got the twelve-month size and while I was at it, picked up the twenty-four month size as well." Bella laughed. "Tommy is actually worried that I might go overboard on baby clothes. Can you imagine?"

Ansley's phone rang. She quickly picked it up, hoping it was Buck. "Davy," she said trying not to sound disappointed since she was the one who'd asked him for the favor.

"If she is the Sadie Montclair of Palm Beach, Florida," Davy said, "then she has quite the mob connection. I found a socialite photo online that tagged her as the goddaughter of Ezra Montclair, Palm Beach business mogul. He's her godfather, all right."

Bella was waving her hand. "Well? Who is she?"

"Any word from the others?" Ansley had to ask before she hung up.

"Nope. Not yet. Don't worry. They know those mountains. They'll be fine."

"Thanks." She disconnected, even more worried. Davy was worried, too, but who wouldn't be given the weather?

"What?" Bella demanded after breathing through another contraction.

"I think we should get you to the hospital," Ansley said, rising. "Your contractions are more consistent and are now ten minutes apart."

Her friend looked surprised that she'd been timing them. "What about Sadie?" she asked as she lumbered to her feet.

Ansley helped her. "Seems Sadie's godfather might be the head of the mob in Palm Beach, Florida."

"Get out of here," Bella cried.

"Which is exactly what we are doing," she said,

steering her toward the door. "Should we call your doctor to let him know we're coming in?"

Bella shook her head. "He's on call. He knows." Her face crumpled. "What if Tommy doesn't make it?"

"I'm sure he'll show up at the hospital as soon as he's out of the mountains," she said, and realized Bella meant what if Tommy doesn't make it out of the mountains. "Do you have a bag packed for the hospital?"

"It's by the door. Tommy insisted."

"I'll grab it." As Ansley picked it up and turned, she saw Bella standing by the door looking back at the house as if she might never see it again.

"Let's go see if this baby is coming today or not," Ansley said too brightly as Bella turned to look at her, tears in her eyes as her water broke.

SADIE TURNED, not sure who she would find standing in the doorway as her hand closed around the grip of the gun. She blinked, startled by the tiny, slim blonde who stared back. But she was more startled by the gun in the angelic-looking woman's hand. She took a wild guess. "Keira."

"Who are you?" the blond woman demanded.

Sadie was debating whether or not she could pull the gun from behind the vase, let alone shoot this woman who DJ considered his little sister. She eased her hand off the grip and pretended to hold on to the mantel for support. "I'm Sadie."

"Sadie, of course. You're that mobster's daughter DJ's been working with down in Florida."

That pretty much summed it up, she thought. Although her father and her godfather considered themselves businessmen who played the odds and used the system to their benefit.

"Where's DJ?" Keira asked, taking in the small cabin and seeing for herself that he wasn't there.

"The last time I saw him, he was headed for the outhouse out back. Actually, I thought you were him returning. He must have heard you coming and took off."

The blonde stepped deeper into the cabin, letting the back door close as she moved away from it. "He wouldn't leave you behind," Keira said, smirking. "I know how he feels about you." Sadie stayed by the fire, turning her back on Keira to warm her hands, and considered her chances if she went for the gun. "Get over here so I can see you."

The gun was in reach, but she could feel the blonde's sights on her back. It was clear that this wasn't the first time Keira had held a gun. There was no reason to believe that she wouldn't use it, Sadie thought as she turned to look at the woman. Sadie had talked herself out of tough spots before, but her instincts told her that trying to reason with this woman would be a waste of breath. There was something in Keira's eyes, something dark, something soulless. She'd seen the look before in some of the men she and DJ had played poker with. It was a terrifying pit to look into, seeing raw greed and hate, knowing there was violence there.

"Sit down," Keira ordered. "In that chair there." She pointed with the gun as she moved closer. "We'll just sit here and wait, although I don't believe he went to the outhouse."

Sadie shrugged as she took the chair as Keira had instructed while her would-be killer stood next to the fireplace wall so she could see both the back as well as the front door. DJ would have heard the snowmobile. He wouldn't just come walking in unaware of what might be waiting for him.

But he would come back to the cabin. He would know it was Keira. He had thought he could leave without facing her. But now that she was here… He wouldn't be able to help himself. He'd want to hear it from her.

Sadie just hoped that this woman didn't kill DJ as he came in the door. Her instincts told her that Keira wouldn't. She would want him to realize what she'd done, for whatever reason. She would want to make him suffer first.

Counting on that, Sadie considered what she could do to stop Keira. Unfortunately, it would be hard to disarm the woman from this chair in front of the fire. Sadie felt tense, waiting for the sound of DJ's boots outside on one of the wooden porch boards. He would be armed, but she really doubted he would fire a weapon before he would ask questions. Keira would know that. Maybe that's what she was counting on.

Sadie caught sight of the Christmas tree DJ had cut for her and they'd had so much fun decorating. They'd laughed so hard as they tried to outdo each other, finding the wildest things to put on that puny tree's limbs. Yet when they'd finished, it looked wonderful to Sadie.

"This is the best real Christmas tree I've ever had," she told DJ.

He'd hugged her and said, "And I thought my childhood was bad."

A sob rose in her throat. She pushed it back down. Now more than ever she needed that poker face that DJ said she was famous for. She couldn't let Keira see what she was feeling. It would make her and DJ more vulnerable.

"He probably went looking for you," Sadie said, wishing it were true. He could have taken off on foot. Or he could still be down digging out the SUV. Now she wished she'd let him take the keys so he could have left in search of his sister. But she doubted he would have. Things had changed between them. She knew DJ was somewhere outside this cabin. He would soon be opening one of the doors and walking into a trap—just as Sadie had feared and Keira had no doubt planned.

BY THE TIME DJ neared the cabin, he could no longer hear the snowmobile's engine. Heart lodged in his throat, he slowed as climbed up to the back door. Sounds in the mountains were often amplified and hard to pinpoint exactly where they were coming from. But there had been no doubt about this earlier sound, he thought as he caught sight of a snowmobile sitting in the pines above the cabin.

He stayed to the trees, keeping the cabin in sight as he approached. He told himself that Sadie was all right. It wasn't like he'd heard anything coming from the cabin. Anything like a scream. Or a gunshot. Yet he knew she was no longer safe, as if his heart now beat in time with hers.

As he reached the side of the cabin, he saw the footprints from the snowmobile sitting in the nearby pines to the back door. He looked around for other tracks. Only one person had gotten off the machine and entered the cabin. Could be PI Crawford.

All his instincts told him it wasn't. Just as he knew it wasn't one of the Grandville men either. The tracks in the snow were too small.

It was Keira.

DJ stood for only a moment considering his best play. He knew the odds. They weren't to his liking. Sadie was in there. He told himself that she was still safe. He would have heard a gunshot. He would have heard a scream. All he heard even now was silence.

Even if Sadie hadn't been inside with Keira, there was no walking away from this. There hadn't been since getting the call drawing him back to Montana. Keira was either here to tell him goodbye before she left for Alaska or she'd come here to earn whatever Grandville had paid her.

He thought about her as a little girl. She'd been so skinny, so pale. He remembered her eyes that first day. He'd had trouble meeting them, afraid of what horrors she'd already been through. Like him, she had no one. Whoever had dropped her off wouldn't be coming back for her and he thought she'd known it.

He'd thought he could protect her, erase whatever had happened to her before Charley's ranch. He'd been a fool. Sometimes you can't save a person. That was a lesson Sadie had never learned.

Tucking the gun into the back of his jeans, he walked to the back of the cabin, hesitated only a moment and opened the door.

Chapter Seventeen

DJ stepped into the cabin. His gaze went to Sadie first. She was sitting in the chair in front of the fire. She gave him a look that said she was all right. He shifted his gaze to Keira, the woman he'd called his little sister since the day she'd arrived at the Diamond Deluxe Ranch.

She stood over Sadie, holding a gun on her. He remembered her wanting to learn to shoot when she was about nine. She'd been so determined that he'd taught her. She'd been a natural, knocking off the cans he'd put on the fence one after another. He remembered the joy in her expression now and felt sick.

When he spoke, his voice was much calmer than he felt. "Keira, want to tell me what's going on?"

"Seems pretty obvious, doesn't it?" she said.

"Sorry, you're going to have to spell it out for me. Talk slowly, you know I never was as quick at catching onto things as you were. Bet you excelled at college."

She shook her head, anger flaring in her eyes.

He feared he'd taken it one step too far. "Right, you worked, you paid for my college. Subtle reminder, big brother. You think that made up for what you did?"

"I'm sorry, what exactly was it that I did, Keira, that you would betray me?" he demanded. "Why would you do this to me? I've always been there for you."

"Not always," she snapped. "You let Charley put me in foster care. You and Charley just left me."

"Keira, I was a kid myself. You were a child much younger than me. There was no way you could have gone with us. That life was no picnic. I was terrified most of the time because people were chasing us, some trying to kill us. There were days when we had nothing to eat, no place to stay but out in the woods."

She shook her head stubbornly. "You abandoned me."

"That's not true. Once I went out on my own, I started sending you money. When it came time for you to go to college—"

"I didn't go to college, DJ. All I ever wanted was what you got—to live the con. I would have been better at it than even you. Look how I conned you."

He stared at her, still disbelieving. "This was Luca's idea, wasn't it?"

"See, that's why you fell for it. You wanted to believe an idea like this could only have come from a man. Keira couldn't have come up with this on her own." She huffed. "It was all my idea, DJ, and it worked." She looked so satisfied that he felt even sicker inside. He'd thought he'd protected her from this life, but he'd been wrong. She'd done this to show him but also to get even for him leaving her all those years ago.

"What did you do with the college money?" he asked.

She smiled. "Taught myself a few tricks of the trade. You wouldn't know, living down there in Florida working for the mob."

"I've been paying off Charley's debt. It's not the glamorous life you think it is." He hated that she'd grown into a hardened woman already, so hard that she'd sold him out to Grandville. "How much do you get for delivering me to them?"

Her smile was all greed and misplaced glory. "Two hundred grand. Like you, Grandville wanted to treat me like a child, or worse, a woman who doesn't know what she's doing. But he sees me differently now."

DJ was sure that Titus did see her differently now. "You can't trust him. He'll turn on you like the venomous snake he is, Keira." But even as he said the words, he could see that she didn't believe him. She'd thought that she'd won Titus Grandville's respect and there was no telling her different.

She tilted her head, listening, but not to him. He heard it too. The whine of snowmobiles in the distance. Grandville was coming with his thugs to get retribution, as if he and his ilk needed a reason. Charley was at the heart of this. Years ago, he remembered his uncle embarrassing Titus on the street in Butte with a card trick. At the time, DJ had looked into the young Grandville's furious red face and worried Titus would go to his father and make things harder for them. He seriously doubted that Titus had ever forgotten the humiliation—or the young threadbare-dressed boy who'd witnessed it. Titus had felt small in front of DJ, a kid he'd ridiculed and felt superior to.

Suddenly DJ felt tired and defeated. He was sick of old grudges and feuds. He'd come up here to save Keira. Worse, he'd gotten Sadie involved. For that, he would never forgive himself. Not that he would have long to regret his mistakes. Titus planned to kill him, but what Keira didn't realize was that the banker wouldn't leave any witnesses.

DJ looked at Sadie. He saw that familiar glint in her eye. She knew the score, but clearly she wasn't ready to give up yet. How had he ever gotten involved with such an optimist?

SADIE HAD TAKEN in the situation. She knew DJ had a weapon on him, but she doubted, even after everything he'd heard, that he was capable of shooting Keira. But Sadie now didn't have that problem. She saw the woman as a product of her own greed, using her childhood as her excuse, blaming everyone but herself for the way her life had turned out so far.

The problem was how to play this and not get DJ or herself killed. She couldn't do anything from this chair, though. She had to take a gamble, something she was apparently born to do.

As she began to clap, Sadie got to her feet to face Keira. "Thank you for this wonderful reminder of how lucky I am not to have a sibling. What a heart-rending moment to have witnessed. To think I used to want a little sister."

Just as she'd hoped, her act caught Keira off guard.

"I told you to sit down there and not move," the woman cried, swinging the gun in Sadie's direction.

Holding up her hands, she'd stepped back toward the fireplace and the gun now within reach behind the vase. She'd also distracted Keira, who was having trouble keeping her gun on both of them.

DJ had moved toward the kitchen, putting the two of them on each side of Keira.

"You move again and I'll shoot you," Keira cried. "That goes for you, too, DJ."

"Other than to get me killed, what is it you want?" he asked, sounding bored.

She took a few steps back, bumping into the bed as she tried to keep them both within sight. "For starters, I want the money you took from the poker game in Butte and any other money you might have on you."

"It's yours," he said. "But I'm going to have to move to get it."

Keira raised the gun so it was pointed at Sadie's head. "Try anything and I kill her."

The sound of the snowmobiles made all three of them freeze for a moment. The sound grew louder, closer. Time was running out. Sadie looked at DJ. *Tell me what you're thinking. Give me a sign.* Otherwise, Sadie was going to do whatever she had to.

THE MOMENT TOMMY and James left in the truck, Buck climbed on one of the snowmobiles, drove it off the trailer and went after Grandville's thugs. He hadn't gone far when he saw the blood on the fresh snow and remembered that James had wounded one of them. A little farther, following the tracks the three had left, he saw a snowmobile sitting without a rider, idling. As he drew closer he saw the body lying next to it on the far side. He cautiously approached. Within a few feet, he saw that it was Lloyd, and he was dead. He appeared to have been shot not once, but twice, the last time between the eyes.

Buck looked to the dark pines ahead, feeling sick to his stomach as he thought about the kind of men he was dealing with. He knew where Rafe and Butch were headed. Charley Diamond's cabin. Were DJ and Sadie there? What about Keira Cross? He gunned his engine; the snow machine roared past the abandoned one as he followed the tracks that he knew would lead him into more trouble than he'd know what to do with.

Ahead, he could see the snowmobile tracks where they had crossed the mountain above the tree line. He'd been following three, now two. But now he saw another track. It, too, had gone in the same direction. His heart sank, as he knew it must belong to the other person on this mountain DJ and Sadie had to fear. Keira.

He just hoped that Tommy and James got word to Willie and the rest of the law in time. He could use all the help he could get since he had a bad feeling Keira had already found DJ and Sadie.

THE BUZZ OF the approaching snowmobiles got louder. DJ could see that Sadie was planning something. He wasn't sure it would make any difference if he was right about who was coming. If it was Grandville's men, they were toast. Keira would be the least of their problems. "You hear those snowmobiles approaching?" he asked his sister, and saw her self-satisfied expression. She thought like he did that they were Grandville's men. "They're going to take the money away from you and kill you. You'll never see the two hundred grand. You'll never see Alaska."

She laughed. "I was never going to Alaska."

"Luca will be so disappointed," he said, wondering if Luca wasn't on one of the snowmobiles headed this way.

"I dumped Luca. He's history. He was just dragging me down. I should have known he'd never get me the start-up money I needed. I realized I'd have to do it myself."

"So you went to Titus. I actually thought he was the one who'd suggested you betray me. But it had been your idea. Good to know. Let me get you that money," he said as he moved toward the bed.

"You can't shame me, DJ," she said angrily. "This life is about doing what needs to be done no matter who it hurts."

He chuckled. "It doesn't seem to be hurting you, Keira. In fact, as smug as you're acting, I get the feeling you're enjoying this."

"So what if I am?" she demanded, waving the gun in his direction as he started across the room.

It was just what Sadie had been hoping for.

SADIE MOVED QUICKLY, deciding at the last moment not to go for the gun behind the vase. She'd already figured out that Keira was cold enough that she might shoot DJ just out of meanness rather than drop her gun. So instead, Sadie went for the woman with the gun.

Even as she launched herself at Keira, she figured the woman would be expecting it. That's why she stayed low, hitting her in the knees, taking her down with a thud that seemed to rattle the entire cabin. Keira managed to get off one shot. Sadie heard it whiz by over her head as she landed on top of the skinny and yet feisty woman. She was already going for the gun when DJ put his boot down on Keira's wrist before she could fire again.

Almost casually, he leaned down and took the weapon from her. Keira kicked at Sadie, grabbing for her hair like a street fighter. Sadie punched her in the face, Keira's head flopping back and smacking the floor. She went still but didn't pass out.

Not that Sadie trusted her. "Please get me something to tie her up with," she said to DJ.

"Let me," he said, handing her the gun as he reached for a dish towel and began to rip it into strips. By the time he'd tied Keira's hands she was kicking and screaming, then pleading with him to let her go. "I'll split the money with you," she cried in desperation.

He shook his head, looking at her with pity. "I don't need the money. I have plenty. I could have paid Titus off without making a dent in my savings."

She stared at him. "Then why didn't you?"

"Because he knew I would try to make the money in a poker game. He would have his ear to the ground making sure that at least one of his men was in the game—and that it would end badly. I wanted to beat him at his own game. Now I wish I'd paid him off and walked away. I won't make that mistake again."

"DJ, let me leave with the money," she pleaded. "I need a new start and you're probably right about Titus double-crossing me."

"Sorry, little sis. It's too late," he said as he dragged her over to a chair and shoved her into it. He appeared to be listening as he tied her to the chair.

Sadie heard it, too. Silence. No sound of the snowmobiles. They both looked toward the back door.

Keira began to laugh. "What did you do to make Titus Grandville hate you so much?"

"Anyone hungry besides me?" DJ asked as he stepped into the kitchen and began to bang around in the pots and pans.

Sadie stared at him and so did Keira. He'd heard the snowmobiles stop on the mountain behind the cabin. Whoever it was had probably already surrounded the cabin. Any moment they would come busting in.

"Sadie, would you mind helping me?" he asked without looking at her.

She moved to stand next to him. "DJ?"

He handed her the opened container of canned meat and a sharp knife, the size that might fit in the top of a boot. "Why don't you cut the ham into slices," he said, still without looking at her. She saw that he had the larger of the two cast-iron skillets on the stove, the grease he'd put in it getting hot.

She glanced behind her at Keira, who was trying to get to her feet as the back door slammed open with a crash. The man in the doorway was big and rough-looking. He was carrying an AK.

"Now isn't this a cute little domestic scene," he said.

"Help me, Butch, they were going to kill me," Keira cried. "Cut me loose," she yelled louder when he didn't move. "I have the money. Hey, I'm talking to you."

Butch started over to the chair and Sadie saw another man standing just outside. He also carried an AK.

"Could you move any slower?" Keira demanded of the thug.

Out of the corner of her eye, Sadie watched Butch walk over to the woman. "Where's the money?"

"I'll get it for you as soon as you untie me," she snapped.

He pulled a knife and began cutting the strips of dish towel from her ankles and wrists.

"Hey, watch it with the knife, you big dumb—"

He raised the butt of the rifle and brought it down hard on her head. The sound reverberated through the small cabin. Sadie's gaze shot to DJ. His eyes were closed; he was gripping the edge of the counter.

"Your sister's taking a nap," Butch said from behind them. "Now where's the money?"

DJ's fingers loosened on the counter. His blue eyes flashed open. "Don't you want breakfast first?" he asked without turning around. His voice sounded strained as he took the ham she'd sliced from her and dumped it into the hot skillet, where it quickly began to sizzle and brown. The skillet was smoking hot. "Toast? What do you think?" he asked Sadie.

Her mouth felt dry. She didn't know what to say, let alone think. DJ was making her nervous. These two thugs were armed with weapons that could saw them in half and he was cooking breakfast?

She heard Butch come up behind them. "I'm sure you're one hell of a chef, but I didn't come here for breakfast, and you know it. Where's the money?" Butch swung the gun toward the front of the cabin and pulled the trigger on the AK, turning the front door into kindling. "Unless you want some of this, you'd better get me my money."

BUCK STOPPED IN the shelter of the trees and shut down his sled. He couldn't hear the two on the snowmobiles in front of him. He figured he must be close to Charley Diamond's cabin because the machines hadn't been silent for long. He could see the trail the two had left to a spot high on the side of the mountain.

As he followed its path, he saw a huge cornice that the blizzard had sculpted high on the peak above the cabin. The cornice hung over this side. He felt a chill.

He'd been caught in a small avalanche as a teenager on a backcountry ski trip. He'd been terrified and fascinated by the power of snow when it started moving. New snow was 90 percent air, yet one foot of it covering an acre weighed more than 250,000 pounds.

In an instant, that cornice could break off and slide. Thousands of tons of snow could come roaring down that mountain at the speed of a locomotive and with the same impact.

He could see the old avalanche chute where trees and rocks had been wiped out next to Charley Diamond's cabin. It wouldn't be the first time a cornice high on the peak had avalanched down. But this time, the cabin might not be so lucky.

The sound of gunfire inside the cabin made him jump as he swung off the snowmachine, lunging through the deep snow. While the snowmobiles had busted a trail, there was still a good two feet of snow below their tracks he had to break through as the gunshots echoed across the mountainside.

Reaching the cabin, he saw three snowmobiles parked outside. Two belonged to Grandville's muscle; the other must belong to Keira since he didn't think DJ and Sadie had brought any.

He moved toward the back door where the machines were parked, weapon drawn, knowing he would be outgunned. Just as he reached the door, all hell broke loose inside.

Chapter Eighteen

The contractions were coming only a few minutes apart when Tommy walked into the hospital room. Ansley felt her heart float up at the sight of him. He went straight to the bed to take his wife's hand. "Heard our girl is coming early," Tommy said, and smiled at Bella, who, in the middle of a contraction, growled at him.

"Buck?" Ansley asked hopefully.

"He's still up on the mountain," Tommy said, his smile fading. "I had to bring James down."

She felt a start. "What happened to James? Is he all right?"

"He's going to live, the doc said." He turned back to his wife. "Lori was on her way up here to check on Bella when I brought James in. She's in the waiting room while he's in surgery. The bullet went straight through. Doc said that was good."

Bella was oblivious to their conversation as she panted through yet another contraction.

"I'll just be down the hall," Ansley told her friend,

and hurried out. James had been shot? Buck was still up on the mountain? She found Lori in the waiting room on the surgical floor.

"What happened?" she cried as she rushed to her.

"James was shot."

"But he's going to be all right?"

"He lost a lot of blood." She sounded close to tears. Ansley was close to them herself. "Willie's headed up there with a helicopter, deputies and EMTs. The Feds aren't far behind, he said."

She nodded but couldn't speak. "I never should have asked them to find my twin," Ansley said.

Lori took her hand. "None of this is your fault. This is what they do."

"You sound like Bella."

"Welcome to being a wife of a private investigator."

"I want to be a wife of a private investigator," Ansley wailed as Lori pulled her into her arms.

"I've known Buck Crawford my whole life," Lori said. "He'll be standing next to you on Saturday. He might be bruised and battered, but he'll be there. Sorry, not funny." She drew back to look at Ansley. "Buck will be there and if there is any way on this earth, your twin brother will be with him."

Ansley desperately needed to believe that finding her missing twin wouldn't cost her everything.

"How's James?"

She looked up to see Davy Colt coming through the door.

"He's in surgery," Lori said.

Davy glanced at his half sister. "Just got the preliminary DNA report from the blood Buck found on that scarf left in his pickup," he said. "DJ Diamond is definitely your twin."

Ansley began to cry. Buck had done just what he'd said he would do—find her missing twin even if it killed him. She couldn't lose them both.

"Settle down," DJ said to Butch as the sound of gunfire died off. "I'll get your money." He knew the money was only an excuse. "Let me take this off the fire." He picked up the pot holder next to the stove, grabbed the handle of the largest skillet and swung around fast.

The sizzling canned ham hit Butch first so he was already screaming when the blistering-hot cast-iron skillet slammed into his face, not once but twice as the AK was wrenched from his hand. The first strike stunned him, the next knocked him to his knees. DJ was about to hit him again when he saw Rafe raising his AK and heard Sadie scream a warning.

Everything seemed to happen too fast after that. DJ saw the winter-clad figure come up behind Rafe. Crawford. The butt end of the PI's handgun came down on the thug's head hard. Rafe dropped, but as he did he pulled the trigger on the AK. Bullets sprayed across the cabin.

When DJ saw what was happening, he grabbed Sadie and threw her down, landing on top of her. As he threw her to the floor, he saw Keira's body jump with each shot before the bullets arced toward him and Sadie on the floor. He'd felt Sadie take one of the bullets even as he tried to shelter her from them. It was as if the bullet punctured his heart. For a moment he couldn't move, couldn't breathe. Beneath him, Sadie wasn't moving, either. His worst fears had come true. He'd gotten Sadie killed.

In the silence that followed, the earth seemed to move. He heard a whump sound, then Crawford yelling. He rolled off Sadie, praying he was wrong, that she was fine. But one look at her and he knew she wasn't. More yelling. He wasn't even sure it wasn't him yelling as he scooped an unconscious Sadie up into his arms.

"We have to get out of here." Crawford was shaking his shoulder. "We have to get out of here. Now!"

He could hear a roar, thinking it was in his ears, but it appeared to be outside as if a runaway train was headed for the cabin.

"This way," Crawford said, dragging him through the demolished front door, off the porch and into the pines away from the cabin. "Keeping going. Don't stop."

He could hear what sounded like trees being snapped off as the roar grew closer. Looking back he could see nothing but a cloud of white. He kept going until Crawford yelled for him to stop. DJ fell to his knees, still holding Sadie in his arms, and the PI rushed to him. Buck took off his coat and spread it on the snow. "Put her down here."

DJ didn't want to let her go.

"Let me check her wound," the PI said.

He slowly released her, laying her on the coat in the snow. He could see that she was still breathing but losing blood from a wound in her side. He stripped off his coat and put it over her, then removed his bloody shirt to press it against her side. He didn't feel the cold. He didn't feel anything as the cloud of snow around him began to dissipate.

"Stay here. I'll get a snowmobile. Help is coming. We just need to get to a spot where a chopper can land," Crawford said.

DJ looked back toward the cabin. It was gone. All he could see was a few boards and one wall sticking up out of the snow farther down the mountain. Charley's cabin was gone and everything in it. Keira. He closed his eyes and pulled Sadie closer as he heard the PI coming with the snowmobile.

Chapter Nineteen

Dressed in his Western suit, Buck rode the elevator up to the recovery floor. He found DJ next to Sadie's hospital bed. He was sitting in a chair, his elbows on his knees, his head in his hands. The anguish he saw there was nothing like what he saw in the man's eyes when DJ lifted his head.

"How is she doing?"

DJ swallowed, nodding, dark circles under his eyes. "The doctor said she should recover—once she's conscious. If she regains consciousness."

"I'm sorry. I know you don't want to leave her, even for a minute," Buck said. "But your twin sister needs you."

DJ shook his head. "She's better off without me. Can't you see that I'm trouble? The people closest to me get hurt. Ansley doesn't need that."

"She needs you, flaws and all. You have no idea how much trouble she's gone through trying to find out the truth about her birth parents," Buck said. "She is no shrinking violet. She's strong. She can handle just about anything, even you." He smiled to soften his words.

"What if my past comes back and I put her life in jeopardy?"

"You'll have family." Buck reached into his pocket, took out the gold bracelet and handed it to DJ. "You'll want this back. Your birth mother had it made for you. She called you Del Junior before you were born, and Ansley DelRae. She wanted you to know your father. You have more than just your twin, though she is definitely a force to reckon with. You're a Colt. You have four half brothers. One's a sheriff, the others are PIs. You also have your birth mother, who is just as anxious to meet you as Ansley is. She didn't know the truth until Ansley came to town looking for her. But you'll hear all about it from your mother, from your twin, from the rest of the family. DJ, you'd be a fool to pass up a chance to be part of this family. You won't be alone. We have you covered."

DJ put his head in his hands for a moment. "I don't want to disappoint her. I've already disappointed two people I swore to protect and got one of them killed."

He could have argued that Keira got herself killed, but he knew that wouldn't help right now. "Believe me, I know what you're feeling. I don't want to let Ansley down, today especially. I promised her I would find you and if at all possible get you to our wedding."

DJ raised his head, took in Buck's suit, and then

looked down at his bloodstained clothing. "Do I look like I'm dressed for a wedding?"

"You will. Like I said, we have you covered. The wedding will be short and once it's over, you can come right back here. Your family is waiting."

"Family, huh." Buck could tell that he was thinking about Keira. "Charley always said you can't overcome your genes," DJ said. "I never knew what that meant until now. Now that my DNA makes me officially a Colt, I guess I don't have much choice."

"You always have a choice," Buck said. "But you'd be a fool to pass up accepting the rest of the Colts as family. Hell, I've been trying to get them to adopt me for years. DJ, I promise I'll have you back here as fast as possible. I brought you some clothes."

"I don't have a present."

"You are the best wedding present either of us will get today. Trust me, once she sees you…"

DJ rose and went to Sadie's side. He leaned down to kiss her forehead, then turned to Buck. "I need to meet my twin before the wedding," he said. "I know you ran the DNA test, and it proves I'm her brother, but I need to know here." He tapped his chest just over his heart.

Buck nodded, hearing the determination in his soon-to-be brother-in-law's voice. "You got it. She can't wait to meet you, either."

ANSLEY STARED INTO the mirror. Today was her wedding day. Brushing her dark hair back, she promised herself she wouldn't cry even as her eyes filled with tears.

"You are going to ruin your makeup," her mother said, and handed her a tissue. "Buck will show. Nothing on this earth can keep him from marrying you today."

She took the tissue, dabbed at her eyes and nodded. "I know it's bad luck to see each other on your wedding day but—"

"Buck called you. He told you he made it out of the mountains. He's going to be here."

"Have you heard how James is doing?" Ansley asked.

"He came through surgery fine. The doctor said he was lucky. The bullet missed vital organs. It was just the loss of blood they were worried about, but you know Lonesome. Once word was out that blood was needed, people turned out to help. Bella and the baby are doing great. It's all good news."

She shook her head. When she'd talked to Davy, he'd told her that Willie and deputies from the sheriff's department had gone up to help search for bodies. Buck could have been one of them. She still worried that he'd been injured and didn't want to tell her. "I shouldn't have put so much pressure on Buck to find my brother. What was I thinking? Me and my perfect Christmas wedding. Without Buck—"

"Oh, honey." Her mother took her in her arms. "Buck will be here and if I know him, he'll have your twin brother with him. That man will move heaven and earth to give you the wedding you've always wanted." She drew back to look at her daughter. "You just have to believe."

Ansley nodded. She did believe in Buck, trusted him with the rest of her life. But she was set to get married in less than an hour and there had been no word from Buck since that one phone call. She couldn't help being terrified that something horrible had happened up there, that she would die alone because Buck Crawford was the only man for her.

Her cell phone rang. She grabbed it up. "Buck?"

"Hey, honey."

"Are you all right?" she cried.

"I'm fine. I'll tell you all about it when I see you. Actually, after the wedding, if that's okay. I know I'm calling it close." Tears of relief began streaming down her face. "There's someone here who wants to meet you before the wedding. He's right outside."

She heard the tap at the door and quickly wiped at her tears, her mother handing her another tissue. The door opened and standing there was her twin brother. She would have known him anywhere. Their gazes met and locked. As tears filled his eyes, she began to cry in earnest as she ran into his arms.

Chapter Twenty

DJ was beside Sadie's bed when she opened her eyes. She blinked, her eyes focusing on his face for a moment before she said, "Tell me you made it to the wedding."

He laughed; it felt good. Sadie was awake. She was going to make it. He couldn't remember ever feeling this overjoyed. "You just made my day and I've already had the most amazing day."

She smiled. "Tell me." She sounded weak, but back from wherever she'd been. He never wanted to come that close to losing her ever again.

So he told her about wanting to see Ansley before the wedding. "It was…incredible," he said, his voice cracking. "I was afraid. I didn't know what to expect. I had no idea what she was like and yet when I saw her…" He shook his head. Sadie reached for his hand, squeezing it, tears glistening in her eyes.

"She told me that she always felt as if a part of her was missing," he said after a moment. "I understood at once. How can a person yearn for something they didn't even know existed? I realized at the cabin that I'd tried to fill that need with Keira. The problem was, she never saw me as family. She never felt the immediate closeness I felt when I saw my twin. It was like a bolt of lightning."

"And the wedding?"

He chuckled. "Of course you'd want to know about that. It was perfect. All of the Colts were there except for James, who's still recovering. I'll fill you in later. But Lori had him on her phone so he got to be there via the internet. I met all my half brothers."

"And your mother?"

He nodded. "It was strange. She's nice. Buck was right. I like all of them. They made me feel like… family."

She smiled. "I figured as much."

"It's a complicated story about my mother and father. He was Del Ransom Colt, one hell of a bronc rider and one hell of a private eye, according to the family. I was named for him. Del Ransom Jr., thus the DJ. Apparently, I come from a long line of rodeo cowboys." Sadie laughed, then winced in pain. "You need to rest."

"So do you. I'm so glad you made the wedding."

"Me, too." She squeezed his hand and closed her eyes. He stayed there watching her breathe, thinking about everything. He didn't move until the sheriff popped his head in and motioned that he was needed out in the hall.

He kissed Sadie on the forehead and went out to

talk to his half brother Willie Colt. They'd met on the mountain in passing.

"How is she?"

"She's conscious," DJ said. "The doctor said she should have a complete recovery."

"Good," Willie said. "I'm going to need to ask both of you some questions about what happened up on that mountain. If now isn't a good time for you…"

"No, I'd just as soon get it over with."

AFTER DJ LEFT her hospital room, Sadie found herself in tears. She hardly ever cried. But seeing DJ, seeing the change in him since meeting his twin and the rest of the family, filled her heart with joy. It would take him a while to get used to it. He'd already lost so much. It would be hard for him to accept this gift of family, but in time, he would and he'd be better for it.

Sadie thought of the pain she'd seen in his eyes on the helicopter ride to the hospital. He'd held her hand, begging her to stay awake. "I can't lose you," he said again and again, his voice rough with emotion, his blue eyes swimming in tears. "I can't lose you."

She remembered little after that until she opened her eyes and saw DJ beside her bed wearing a Western suit and bolo tie. He looked so handsome in the suit, so different from the Montana cowboy she'd known. Wiping her tears, she closed her eyes, surprised how exhausted she felt.

When she woke again, her room was filled with

women all about her age. They introduced themselves as Carla, Davy's wife; Ellie, Willie's wife; Lori, James's wife; and Bella, Tommy's wife. The Colt women had brought her gifts, wanting to meet her. Ansley was with them.

"Shouldn't you be on your honeymoon?" Sadie had asked.

"Buck and I aren't going anywhere until all of you are out of the hospital," the pretty dark-haired woman told her. "It's my fault since I desperately wanted my twin at the wedding. I could have gotten you all killed."

Sadie shook her head. "Your search for DJ actually saved our lives. We wouldn't be here now if it wasn't for your husband."

Bella had just given birth to a little girl with dark hair and Colt blue eyes. "She's precious," Sadie said after looking at the photo, since the infant was still down the hall in the nursery after coming a month early.

The women were fun, laughing and bringing cheer to the hospital room. They were all so excited about DJ being found, commenting on how much he looked like Ansley.

"We brought you a few things you might like," Lori Colt told her.

Bella had produced a dusty-rose-colored nightgown. "DJ said dusty rose was your color. I promise it's more comfortable than a hospital gown."

They also brought her flowers, candy, lip balm,

lotion, a scented candle. They promised that their next visit they'd bring ice cream and small fried pies from Lori's former sandwich shop.

True to their word, they showed up the next day with the treats and lots of laughter and stories, often about the Colt brothers and growing up around Lonesome.

Sadie couldn't imagine, not after growing up in Palm Beach. Here the mountains came right down to the small western town. Pine trees grew everywhere. She wondered what it was like when it wasn't covered in a thick blanket of snow. She thought about what DJ had said about his favorite season, spring in Montana. She had never lived in a place that had seasons.

"How is DJ doing?" she'd asked. She didn't need to explain herself. They knew at once what she was asking since they knew that he had practically been camped out at the hospital.

"It's like he's always been part of the family," Carla, Davy's wife, said. "I think at first he was nervous, but once he met his brothers, I think he realized how much they all have in common."

"If you're asking if he plans to stay," Bella said, always the one to get to the heart of things, Sadie had realized, "he knows he's welcome. The brothers told him that there's a section of the ranch that is his for a house, if he wants it. They also told him that the ranch is as much his as theirs. I heard them talking about raising more cattle."

"It's the way Del would have wanted it, all of his offspring together," Lori said.

"I'm sure DJ is overwhelmed by all of your generosity. I certainly am," Sadie said, wondering why DJ hadn't mentioned any of this to her. Because he was going to turn it down? Or because he was going to take their offer? Probably because it was all overwhelming and he hadn't made up his mind yet.

"Bet you're ready for a nice juicy burger," Carla said. "We'll bring you one tomorrow."

"When are you blowing this joint?" Bella inquired. "We want you and DJ to come out to the ranch for dinner. I'm also throwing a New Year's Eve bash if you feel up to it by then."

"We've worn her out enough for one day," Lori said. "She doesn't have to make any big decisions right now."

"Except about the burger," Ellie said. "You want that loaded?"

She laughed and nodded. "Fries?"

"Of course fries," Bella cried. "What do you think we are?"

They'd all left laughing and Sadie found herself looking forward to their next visit even as she realized the visits would soon be ending. The doctor said she was healing nicely and would be able to leave soon—long before New Year's Eve.

TITUS GRANDVILLE HATED his father butting into his business. Worse was when his old man showed up unannounced at his office. He'd had no word on what had transpired up in the mountains. Butch had promised to call the moment it was done. He hadn't called. The storm had stopped. The plows were running, the roads opening up.

Nerves on end already, looking up and seeing Marcus walk in only angered him. "What are you doing here?"

His father didn't answer, merely came in, pulled out a chair and sat down across the desk from him.

"Hello?" Titus snapped. "I really don't need this right now. I'm busy. I have work to do. What are you doing here?"

"This used to be my office," his father said. "You probably don't remember when you and your brother Jimmy used to play on the floor in here. You always took Jimmy's toys."

"Why are we talking about my dead brother?" Titus demanded. He knew his father still blamed him for the car crash that had killed Jimmy. He'd felt enough guilt over it; he didn't need the old man to rub it in, especially today.

"I always wondered why you didn't cry at the funeral."

Titus was on his feet. "Would love to wade through the past with you, Dad, but not today. You need to leave."

"Things didn't go like you planned them, did they?"

He felt the hair rise on the back of his neck. "Why would you say that?"

"Because I saw the cops as I came up the back way."

It was the smugness on his father's face. All of his life, his father had tried to tell him what to do. "You never trusted my instincts," Titus snapped. "Not even once. You never said, 'Good job, son.'"

"You never gave me reason to," Marcus said as two uniformed officers filled his office doorway.

"Titus Grandville?" one of the officers said as he stepped in. "We need you to come with us."

"What's this about?" Titus asked innocently as he saw his father get to his feet.

"We're arresting you for the murder of Keira Cross and attempted murder of DJ Diamond and Sadie Montclair as well as the deaths of Lloyd Tanner, Butch Lamar and Rafe Westfall and the shooting of PI James Colt."

"Is that all?" Marcus Grandville said with a laugh as he moved out of the cops' way.

"You realize that you can't prove any of this, right?" Titus said.

Titus looked around for a way out, his gaze going to his father who was standing back, smiling as if to say, "Told you so." It was something he'd heard all his life. He'd killed the good son, his father's favorite, and Marcus had never let him forget it.

"Enjoying this, old man?" Titus said as one of the cops began reading him his rights and the other cuffed him. Soon he would be doing the perp walk through the Grandville building out to a squad car. "You've been waiting for this day, haven't you?"

His father nodded, then grimaced, his hand going to his chest as he fell back against the wall and slumped to the floor. One of the cops hurried to him and quickly called 911 to report that the elderly man appeared to be having a heart attack.

"Go ahead and take him down to headquarters," the cop said to the other cop as he began to do CPR on Marcus.

Titus stared at his father, wondering why the cop was bothering. "You're wasting your time. He has a bad heart. It's rotten to the core. There's no saving him."

The cop jerked on his arm, dragging him to the door.

"I want to call my lawyer," Titus said. "I'm going to sue you and the police department for false arrest. You have no proof that I've done anything." On the way out of his office he saw two men in suits coming toward him. The one in the lead flashed his credentials. FBI. He waved a warrant.

"When it rains, it pours," Titus said, and smirked at agents demanding to see all records and confiscating all computers and phones.

Before they reached the street, EMTs raced past them on the way up to the top floor. Titus looked out at dirty snow in the street and told himself he'd be out of jail before the EMTs reached the top floor. He was a Grandville, the last of them, finally. All of this was his. He was finally taking his rightful place. These people had no idea who they were dealing with.

WHEN SADIE WOKE later that evening, the nurse told her that she had another visitor. She was glad to see Buck Crawford enter her room. "I heard you were getting better. I had to see for myself."

She smiled at him, sitting up a little. She knew little of what had happened up on the mountain. DJ had glossed over it when she'd questioned him on one of his many visits. Clearly, he hadn't wanted to relive it—not that she could blame him. "Tell me what happened after I was shot. It's all such a blur." She listened as he told her about the avalanche.

"Keira?" Buck shook his head. "She took one of the bullets. She was gone before the cornice broke and fell. We barely got you out before the avalanche hit the cabin. Her body will be recovered and when it does, DJ said he plans to have her buried next to Charley Diamond on the mountainside cemetery back in Butte."

"And the Grandvilles?" she asked.

"Titus was arrested earlier today in Butte. One of the men from the poker game, Keith Danson? He's turning state's evidence against Titus. He might never get out of prison. The FBI has been investigating him for some time apparently. They raided his office earlier. I suspect whatever they find added to murder and attempted murder…" He shrugged. "I'd say the reign of the Grandvilles is over, since his father died of a heart attack during Titus's arrest."

Sadie shook her head. It all sounded too familiar. "How is DJ?" she finally had to ask.

"He won't have any trouble with the law," Buck said. "Both Butch Lamar's body and Rafe Westfall's bodies have been retrieved from the avalanche. I'm sure their connection to Titus Grandville will be of interest to the Feds, but DJ is in the clear."

"So it's over," Sadie said, thinking of DJ.

"It doesn't have to be," Buck said as if reading her thoughts.

She smiled, wishing it were true. She was DJ's past. These people and this town, they were his future. He'd come by the hospital constantly to see how she was doing. Each time, she asked about his new family and each time, he would smile and tell her. She saw that he was indeed overwhelmed by their acceptance and even more so by their love.

When the doctor told her that she was being released in a few days, she knew it would be best if she didn't see DJ again once she left. He had to learn a lifetime about himself, about his mother and his father, about the family he had only recently found. But he was fortunate that he had people to tell him the stories, to fill in the gaps in his life, to share memories of his father. He also had his mother, who was now part of the Colt family circle. She, too, had missed out on so much, but at least she'd gotten to watch the Colt brothers grow up.

Sadie had no idea what DJ's future held—just that he needed to sort it all out. She wanted him to have this time. They both needed it. She could admit it now. She loved DJ Diamond and always would. Which was why she couldn't say goodbye. It would hurt too bad. She also knew that he would try to get her to stay and she might if he asked. She couldn't imagine ever loving anyone as much as she did him. Her heart couldn't take a long goodbye.

On the day she was to be released, the nurse came in to tell her that she couldn't leave until a wheelchair was brought up for her. "Then please hurry," Sadie had said. "I have a plane to catch." The nurse gave her a disapproving look but turned and left.

Sadie pulled out her phone and called her godfather before she could change her mind. It was a call she'd been putting off and was grateful when he didn't answer. She left a voice mail. "Headed home. Will see you soon."

Chapter Twenty-One

DJ told himself that he was ready to look toward the future as he hurried up to Sadie's floor at the hospital. Yesterday, he'd put Keira to rest in the cemetery next to Charley. He still couldn't help feeling as if he'd failed her even though he knew Charley would have told him that it all came down to genes.

He'd been rediscovering his own genes. He was a Colt from his dark hair to his blue eyes. The more he was around his twin and his half brothers, the more he saw himself in them. They'd taken a different path in life, but they weren't that different. The Colt brothers risked their lives at their jobs—just as they'd risked them in the rodeo. It seemed something in their blood craved adventure. They were all gamblers at heart.

Pushing open Sadie's hospital room door, he couldn't contain his excitement. He couldn't wait to tell Sadie what he had planned. He'd never bought flowers for a woman before, and he felt uncomfortable holding the large bouquet. There was so much he had to say to her, words that had been stacking up, ready to burst out of him since he'd admitted how he felt about her.

Just the thought terrified him. He'd told Sadie that he loved her at the cabin, something he'd never said to another woman because he'd never felt love like that before her. Over the time they'd worked together they'd become more than colleagues. They'd become friends. It was no wonder that he'd fallen for her.

But she'd never taken him seriously. She thought he chased more women than he did. He'd let her believe it, a mistake, he realized some time into their relationship. From the beginning, she'd made it perfectly clear that it was hands-off. If he needed a reminder there was her godfather, who'd also warned him with the threat of violence not to fall in love with Sadie. Their arrangement had been strictly business.

Until Montana. Until they were snowed in at the cabin high in the mountains just before Christmas. Until they'd let their true feelings out.

Now, though, they had to decide about their future. He knew what he wanted, but he wasn't sure Sadie would. He knew that wouldn't be a deal breaker for him. He loved her. He'd go and do whatever she wanted. It would be hard though to leave Montana, to leave the family he'd found, especially to leave his twin. He and Ansley had bonded instantly.

As he stepped into Sadie's room, he stopped cold when he saw the stripped bed and the woman from housekeeping readying the room for the next patient. For just an instant he thought the worst.

"She…she…tell me she didn't…"

The woman looked up. "Leave? She checked out this morning."

That wasn't possible. "But she wasn't supposed to check out until this afternoon."

"She checked out early."

She'd just checked out without letting him know? "Where did she go?"

The woman shrugged. "You might ask downstairs."

He looked down at the bouquet of flowers. "That's you, Diamond, a dollar short and a day late," he whispered to himself as he turned around and left the room. Uncle Charley used to say that when he messed up. He'd really messed up this time.

Downstairs he inquired as to where Sadie Montclair had gone and found out that she had been trying to catch a flight to Florida. Without saying goodbye? Maybe something urgent had happened to her godfather. Otherwise… Otherwise, she'd gone home, back to Florida, back to the life she was born into. Their partnership over, she felt there was nothing keeping her in Montana?

He thought about their time together in the cabin. His chest felt hollowed out, his heart crushed. She'd said she loved him. Clearly, she'd changed her mind. Otherwise, why would she just leave without even saying goodbye?

It wasn't like he'd asked her to stay, he reminded himself. But how could he? He not only had little to offer her, but also he'd put her life in danger and might again if she stayed with him. Wasn't it better to let her walk away? It wasn't like he was a prize. Why would she want to marry him?

"What are you doing?"

He recognized the voice calling to him. As he came out of the hospital, he turned to see Buck Crawford on his way in. "Shouldn't you be on your honeymoon?" he asked Buck.

"Ansley postponed it until we knew that James and Sadie were going to be okay. Wasn't Sadie being released this afternoon?"

"Apparently she left early. She's gone."

"I take it you missed her. So go after her," Buck said.

DJ hesitated, feeling lost. "She apparently already made her decision about me."

Buck sighed. "I'm going to give you some unsolicited advice, brother-in-law. When you find the woman who makes you doubt everything about yourself and at the same time makes you believe you're superhuman, you hang on to her."

He shook his head. "I'm not sure she feels the same way."

"One way to find out," Buck said. "Press your luck. Love is a gamble, but when you win…" He broke into a huge grin.

As he started to go inside, DJ said, "Did Ansley send you?"

His brother-in-law just laughed. "She said it's a twin thing."

SADIE HAD PLANNED to take a taxi home, so she was surprised when her godfather picked her up at the airport.

"Is everything all right?" she had to ask as she climbed into the back of the town car beside him.

"That's what I want to know," he said. "When I heard you were flying home, I was worried."

"I'm fine. The doctor said I will have a scar but other than that…"

He took her hand. "I'm sorry."

She turned slowly to look at her godfather, frowning in confusion.

"I shouldn't have brought DJ Diamond into your life."

Sadie shook her head. "I was the one who followed him to Montana."

"When I met him, I knew he was trouble. I just thought the two of you would be a good match. I had no idea that you would fall for him."

"I never said I—"

"You don't have to. I know you, Sadie. What I want to know now is what are you going to do about it?" She stared at him. "Don't tell me that you're going to let him get away with breaking your heart."

"It wasn't like that. I was the one who left. It's better this way."

"For whom? You look like someone kicked your dog. You've never backed down from a challenge. Why are you running now?"

Sadie shook her head, thinking about the small cozy cabin, making love in front of the fire with the snow falling outside. It had been magical—but it hadn't been real life. It was a fantasy few days in a snowstorm. To read any more into it was beyond foolish.

"Please don't insult my intelligence by trying to tell me that you aren't still in love with him."

"Even if I was, I can't believe you'd want me to marry him," she said, shocked by this conversation. "You're the one who warned me not to fall in love with him."

Her godfather shook his head. "But you did anyway and now you come back here looking like you let him steal your heart and you're afraid to go get it back. No goddaughter of mine would give up so easily."

"I'm your only goddaughter." She frowned. "Aren't I?"

He smiled, something he seldom did. "You are indeed. Does he love you?"

How did she answer that? She thought of him beside her hospital bed. She thought of the way he'd looked in her eyes, the way he'd held her, kissed her, made love to her. But how did she know that she was any different from the other women DJ had seduced?

As if reading her mind, her godfather said, "Don't be a fool. That cowboy has been smitten with you from the start. But if you don't believe it, go back there and ask him. He'd be a fool if he wasn't and DJ Diamond is a lot of things, but he's not a fool."

"You make it sound so simple."

"Love?" He chortled a laugh. "It's the most complicated and confusing, excruciatingly painful and exasperating emotion there is. But it's what makes life worthwhile. Stop being a coward and find out how that man feels about you. How can it be any worse than the way you're feeling right now?"

"Want to tell me about the woman who broke *your* heart?" she asked.

"No, I don't," he snapped. "And Sadie? Take the private jet, if you want. And if he says he doesn't love you, shoot him. I have people who will take care of the body."

"I wish you were joking," she said, but had to smile. "Thank you."

DJ COULDN'T BELIEVE it when he got the text from Sadie.

I'm sorry I left the way I did. I love you. If you can forgive me, I'll be flying into Yellowstone International Airport tomorrow afternoon at 4. I'll be the one wearing the red cowboy boots.

He read the text twice. He'd really thought that he'd never hear from her again. He'd been telling himself that he had to let her go. A part of him believed that she loved him, but maybe love couldn't conquer all—no matter what his twin said. His heart had been breaking since finding her gone. Now he was almost afraid to trust she'd be back again.

Except this was Sadie. This was the woman he loved. He'd had to let her go even though he'd been planning to go after her. He read the message again—just in case he'd misread it.

He smiled and tried to still his pounding heart before he responded with his own. I'll be wearing my hat.

Then he headed for the airline ticket counter to cancel his flight to Florida that was leaving in an hour. Sadie loved him. His smile was so big it hurt his face. Sadie loved him. Love had brought her back. Just as love had him wearing his lucky boots as he planned to fly to Florida and try to get her back.

Okay, maybe Ansley was right. Maybe love could bring two very different people together. Just as it had brought him to this family of his. He pulled out his phone. He couldn't wait to tell his twin.

"Didn't I tell you that nothing can stop true love?" Ansley cried. "You two were meant for each other. It is high time you told her what's in your heart. But first here's what we need to do."

SADIE WORE HER red cowboy boots. The first time she met DJ, he'd been wearing a pair of worn cowboy boots. She'd commented on them, suggesting he buy a new pair.

He'd laughed. "Sorry, sweetie, but these are my lucky boots."

"Call me sweetie again and not even your lucky boots can save you."

She could laugh about it now. Especially since she was wearing her boots because she needed all the luck she could get as she got off the plane.

"He needs time with you and the rest of his family," she'd told Ansley when she'd called.

"He needs you. He loves you and you love him. That makes you family. You need to come back. He's hurting."

"So am I."

"Do you love him?"

"I do." Her voice had cracked. "I just don't know where we go next."

Ansley had laughed. "You think there's a road map? It's a leap of faith. None of us can see the future. We just have to believe that something amazing is ahead and enjoy each day. DJ told me you were an optimist."

"He did, did he?"

"All he talks about is you," Ansley said. "He wants to make a life with you. He has a plan."

She'd laughed. She was familiar with his plans. "A plan?"

"He'll tell you all about it when he sees you. He isn't going to let you go. My brother is no fool, even though sometimes he acts like one." They'd laughed. "Tell me you'll give him a chance. You know he loves you."

She did know, she thought as she looked around for DJ in the crowd at the Yellowstone International Airport. She spotted him standing against a nearby wall, his Stetson cocked on his dark hair, those blue eyes taking her in as if she was a cold drink of water in the desert. He pushed off the wall and headed toward her as she descended the stairs.

The way she'd left without saying goodbye and having been gone for a couple of days, she thought they'd be awkward with each other. That they no longer had anything to say. That they would realize not even love could sustain this relationship.

She watched him approach, her pulse hammering.

"Sadie." That one word filled her heart like helium. DJ looped his arm around her waist and picked her up before she reached the bottom step. He swung her around, taking her in his arms as he put her down. For a moment, he just looked at her, then he kissed her passionately.

She heard cheers and clapping, but they were a distant sound. Her heart was beating too loudly in her ears as DJ drew back.

"I love you, Sadie Montclair. Marry me." He dropped to one knee. "Love your boots, by the way," he whispered, then said, "Be my wife, be my partner, be mine."

She smiled. She knew this man. This wasn't such a leap of faith. Yet she couldn't speak as she looked into his eyes. All she could do was nod and fall into his arms as he rose. There were more cheers and clapping than before as some of the crowd joined in along with the entire Colt and Crawford clan.

All she could think was that from now on these would be her lucky boots as she was swept up in this large, gregarious, loving family.

Did it matter what the future held? Not as long as she and DJ faced it together. She was putting her money on the two of them. It wasn't a safe bet, but she was ready to play the odds.

Chapter Twenty-Two

It was their first Christmas holiday together. Also their first with DJ's family. Sadie had never seen anything like it and she could tell that DJ was just as overcome by it all. The Colts had a variety of holiday traditions—including all getting together at Bella and Tommy's because they had the largest space. There was a mountain of food and holiday treats, games and prizes, and more presents than she'd ever seen.

Because of everything that had happened, even the holiday had been put off until they could all be together.

"Ansley," Buck cried as he finished bringing in all the presents his new bride had purchased.

"I might have gone a little overboard," she admitted. "But it's our first Christmas, the first with my family, the first with my twin."

Buck smiled and raised his hands in surrender. "Given all that, I'm surprised you exhibited such self-control."

Sadie and DJ had gone shopping even though everyone told them it wasn't necessary. "The two of you are our presents," Ansley had said, and the others had agreed.

"It's just because you don't know us very well," DJ had joked. "By next year, you'll feel entirely different."

Still, they'd shopped together. It had been fun. Even DJ had enjoyed it. Sadie could tell that he'd never had anyone to buy for, other than Keira, and they'd never celebrated holidays together.

They went to Bozeman, hitting all the shops, and then had lunch in a quaint place along Main Street.

This large, exuberant family was something so new for them both that they grew quiet after they ate. Sadie thought that it was all just starting to sink in. When DJ spoke, she knew he'd been thinking the same thing.

"Can we do this?" he asked, meeting her gaze.

She didn't have to ask what he meant. The two of them, she felt, were solid together because they knew each other given everything they'd been through. "We can do anything we set our minds to."

"Are you sure we aren't too broken?" DJ asked.

Sadie chuckled. "Isn't everyone in one way or another?"

He shook his head. "What worries me is that I really like them. I don't want to let them down. Especially Ansley."

"You won't." She reached across the table to take

his hand. "We have the rest of our lives yet to live. Our pasts are…unique, but they have also made us stronger. We're survivors. We can do this."

He smiled then, squeezing her hand, and she let go. "I've never asked you what you wanted out of life."

"To be like everyone else." She said it quickly and shrugged. "Promise you won't laugh?" He nodded solemnly and crossed his chest above his heart with his finger. "I want a family. I want what the Colt women have."

"To be married to private eyes?"

She shook her head. "They have a sense of community I've never had. They're all excited about their kids growing up together. Bella is convinced the kids will rule the school. I have no doubt hers will." She laughed. "I want Montana." She saw his surprised expression.

"I never thought you'd leave Florida."

"I want to see spring here," she said, glancing toward the restaurant window. Christmas decorations hung from the streetlights. Snow was piled up along the edge of the street. Everyone outside was bundled up against the cold. "I want to see the grass turn green, to feel the sun bring back life. I want to grow a garden and catch a fish out of the river." Her voice broke. "I want an ordinary house with a swing set in my backyard and a couple of kids out there playing on it."

He laughed. "You want a lot," he joked. "Just a couple of kids?"

"I'd discuss more," she said with a grin.

DJ turned serious. "You haven't mentioned this husband of yours."

She smiled. "I want him to be anything he wants. Lover, father, best friend. You want to raise cattle to go with that Stetson of yours, I'm all for it."

His eyes seemed to light up. "My brothers want to make the Colt Ranch a true ranch. There's plenty of land and they've offered me a section for our house. I have money to buy whatever we'll need."

"You know I have my own money, so we can pretty much do anything we want." She met his gaze, her heart in her throat. Was it possible? Could they do this? "Wouldn't you miss the grift?"

"Sounds like raising cattle might be enough of a gamble."

"I'm serious. You love what you do."

"I used to, but I've lost my taste for it. I'm like you. I look around Lonesome and I feel the need to put down roots. I want a swing set in my backyard. I want a couple of blond towheads out there who look just like you but are trying to see how much higher they can swing. You do realize that if you and I had kids they'd get some of my genes."

She smiled. "Would that be so bad? I happen to love your jeans. Especially the way they fit you."

He locked eyes with her. "We could do this, you

and me. We could make a good life here in Montana. You'd have to learn to ride a horse."

"You know how to ride? You never told me that."

"I was raised on a ranch."

"Charley had a horse?"

"A couple of wild ones that Keira and I used to try to ride." At the mention of Keira a shadow crossed his face for a moment. "Our kids will have horses. Apparently rodeoing is in my blood."

"So I've heard. Let's cross that bridge when we get to it," she said. "But I'd love to have a horse of my own. Bella rides all the time. I know she'd teach me."

He nodded. "I can see us here."

"Me, too." She felt her smile widen. "I love you, DJ. I have for a very long time. You do realize that my godfather will want to give me away."

"Yes, your godfather. You sure he's good with this, you and me?"

She nodded. "He gave me his blessing." She didn't mention what else he'd said as DJ leaned across the table to steal a quick kiss.

They both grinned. They'd found not only their way to each other, but to a family and a place to make a home and a life neither of them had ever expected.

They could do this. Together. Partners forever.

JUST BEFORE MIDNIGHT on New Year's Eve, Sheriff Willie Colt stood, raising his glass as he looked around the table. As the oldest of the Colt brothers and prodded by his wife Ellie, it was up to him to speak before they rang in the new year. Bella and Tommy had thrown quite the party as usual. The whole family was here, and it had grown considerably since last year.

"It's been quite the year, wouldn't you say?" Everyone laughed.

"What a couple years this has been," Willie said as he looked around the huge table. "When James got hurt on his last bronc ride and came home, we all expected him to do what we usually did, heal up and go back. But instead he started digging into Dad's last case, the one he'd never solved before his death. We couldn't have known where that was going to lead."

There were murmurs around the table. "James gave up rodeoing to reopen Dad's private investigative business. It was the beginning of Colt Brothers Investigation. Tommy was lured back and then Davy. I was determined not to join this ragtag bunch," he said, and laughed.

"Instead, I joined the sheriff's department as a deputy to find out what had really happened to Dad that night when he was killed on the railroad tracks. I ended up finding something that I loved more than rodeo, law enforcement, and that led me to Seattle, and we all know how that ended."

More laughter around the table.

"We got Ellie," Bella said, and the other women all joined in with cheers. "Turned out to be a great deal."

"It wasn't like we ever expected you to fall in love, let alone get married," James said.

"We figured you would be Lonesome's old cranky bachelor," Tommy said.

"He's still cranky," someone said.

Willie waited until the laughter died down. "The four of us are now married, some of us fathers. There's been a few surprises along the way." He looked in the direction of Ansley and DJ and smiled. "Happy surprises," he added. He watched Ansley hug her brother and Sadie, tears in her eyes.

"We hadn't wanted to believe Dad's pickup being hit by the train was an accident. We now know it was. Also, we learned a lot about our mother, who was a mystery to us all." He glanced down the table at Beth. "I know Dad loved our mother, Mary Jo, but I also know that she made his life very hard. He found true love the second time with Beth, Ansley and DJ's mother. Sometimes we don't get the happy endings we want, but in the end we're so thankful for family. I wish Dad were here to see this. I like to think he'd be proud. I know I am at what you've all accomplished."

He cleared his voice. "Now we're about to start another year and I for one can't wait to see what this amazing family has in store for it." A cheer went up. He looked over at his wife. Ellie was glowing.

"Are you kidding me?" Bella cried. "Ellie?"

Her sister-in-law smiled and nodded. "There is a little Willie in the works." That brought on more cheering along with groans from some of the brothers and remarks like, "Never thought you had it in you, bro."

"It's almost time," someone called out, and everyone looked to the clock on the wall. They rose from the table as the countdown began. "Ten, nine, eight, seven…" The joy in the room rose as their voices joined to ring in the new year.

"Six, five, four, three, two… Happy New Year!"

Willie took Ellie in his arms and kissed her. All around him he watched his brothers and their wives and girlfriends kiss and hug. Noisemakers came out and confetti filled the air along with balloons. Bella never did anything halfway, he thought. This year she had a lot of help from the family since she had a new baby girl.

Willie laughed, hoping his father was watching all of this. This was the family he'd started. Willie hoped he'd be proud.

Epilogue

Ansley felt as if her feet weren't touching the ground as she looked out past the American flag flapping in the backyard breeze to her husband standing with the Colt men by the barbecue grill. Her husband. She would never get tired of staying that.

"You have been smiling way too much for a woman about to turn thirty," Bella said as she put her daughter down in the playpen in the shade. Daisy immediately began cooing and waving her arms at the bird mobile hanging over her head. Her twin boy cousins were in another playpen, also in the shade. Both were sacked out. Their older sister, Jamie, was playing in the kiddie pool not far from where the men were grilling lunch.

"Isn't it wonderful to have so much family?" Ansley said, knowing that Bella had also been an only child. So had Lori and Carla and Ellie. Probably why all of them wanted numerous children. "Just think, Daisy will grow up with all these cousins. Won't that be fun?" Carla and Ellie were both pregnant. When

Ansley had gone looking for her birth mother she could never have imagined finding this much family.

"Don't try to change the subject." Bella looked down to where Tommy was standing. As if feeling her gaze on him, he looked up and smiled. She smiled back and glanced down at their daughter. Ansley knew Bella had to be thinking about how close she'd almost come to losing him the day their baby was born.

"What's going on with you?" Bella said. "I can tell you're holding out on me."

Ansley smiled as she saw her twin standing with the other men. Just the sight of DJ brought her such joy. She'd been so afraid that they would never find him and when Buck had, she'd been so afraid that she would lose them both. When he'd walked in before her wedding…

Tears filled her eyes at the memory. She made a swipe at them, embarrassed at how emotional she'd been lately. "I'm happy, that's all," she said. "I love my life and you're a part of that."

Bella made a rude sound. "Okay, fine. Just keep it to yourself, but I have to tell you, you should never play poker. Your face gives everything away."

She laughed as she scanned Bella's backyard. Soon she would have a backyard of her own. Her brothers and Buck's father and brother had been helping with the new houses being built on the Colt Ranch for her and Buck—and for DJ and Sadie. She couldn't wait until theirs was finished.

Past the men at the barbecue grill, Lori and Ellie

were uncovering the salads and desserts on the table under the umbrella. Sadie was busy putting serving spoons in everything. Ansley could tell they were laughing and was amazed how Sadie had become one of them so quickly. Having all of these women come into her life was a joy she'd never anticipated when she'd come looking for her birth mother.

Speaking of her birth mother, where was she? Running late probably, because she was working even on a holiday. Being the mayor of Lonesome was a full-time job, one Beth took seriously—just as she did motherhood. She was going to make a wonderful grandmother. Ansley started to go help with the other women when Bella stopped her.

"Ansley!" Bella demanded. "No one is this excited for her thirtieth birthday, not even you."

She couldn't help but smile. Her happiness just seemed to overflow these days. "It's my birthday! Mine and DJ's. It also just happens to be the Fourth of July." They were also celebrating Davy's birthday as well since his was only a few days ago.

Bella was giving her a side-eye when suddenly her eyes widened. "Oh, you are not." She was laughing and smiling. "Does Buck know yet?"

"No, and don't you dare tell him. I want to surprise him tonight during the fireworks show."

Her friend's eyes filled with tears. "I am so happy for you. So happy for all of us. I never imagined that our children would be raised together on this ranch. We're all going to get sick of each other," she joked.

She pulled her into a hug. "I'm so glad you came

into our lives and brought DJ and Sadie. You know they'll be getting married soon. I love weddings. Can you imagine what it is going to be like when all of our kids go to school?" Bella asked as she looked down at her daughter, who'd fallen asleep. "The Colt kids will rule the school. Along with the Crawfords and Diamonds, of course. The teachers won't know what hit them."

Ansley saw Buck look up at her. Their gazes met and she realized that he knew. He gave her a wide grin. So much for waiting until the fireworks. They'd already had their fireworks and now they were going to have a baby.

DJ PULLED SADIE ASIDE. "It's not too late. You can change your mind about marrying me." He waved a hand, taking in all the family gathered today. "I suspect it will always be like this."

"I certainly hope so," she said, stepping into his arms. "Happy birthday." She kissed him and let him lead her into the cool of the pines and out of sight of the others.

He held her at arm's length as he studied her. "I wouldn't be here if it wasn't for you. I almost lost you because of it."

She shook her head. "We *are* here now. Together. There is no looking back anymore. You changed my life…don't you realize that?"

DJ smiled. "How did I ever get so lucky?"

"I guess you played to your strengths."

"Whatever the reason, thank you for being my

partner. I'm sure you had your doubts when your godfather suggested we work together."

Sadie laughed. "It was when I met you that I really had my doubts. What was I supposed to do with this arrogant Montana cowboy?"

"Save him from himself," DJ said, and pulled her closer for another kiss.

"Do you think we could sneak away during the fireworks show?" he asked.

"You're incorrigible," she said with a laugh.

"I just can't seem to get enough of you." He kissed her and drew back. "Okay, we should go back to the barbecue. Everyone will be talking about us."

"Everyone is already talking about us. They wonder what a man like you is doing with a woman like me."

He drew her close again so that their bodies were molded together. "I hope you told them "

Laughing she pulled away. "I love your family."

"*Our* family. They are pretty fantastic, aren't they? Ansley is nothing short of amazing. Do you know that she started her own jewelry business without the help of her rich family? Talk about determination."

Sadie nodded, smiling. "She's a lot like her twin. She just wouldn't give up hope that Buck would find you and bring you to the wedding."

"Thanks to you I made it. I wish you could have been there."

"All that matters is that you made it and just in time."

"You know me, I like to call things close to the wire," DJ said.

"Yes, I do know that about you."

He met her gaze. "I'll be early to our wedding. Are you sure you want to be the wife of a rancher? Us living on the Colt Ranch. Me, raising cattle."

"After all those years of being all hat and no cattle?" she joked. "I suspect you were born to ranching. You love a gamble."

He grinned. "You know me so well."

"Don't I, though," she said as he put his arm around her waist and led her back toward the barbecue and their new family.

"Your godfather still coming to our wedding this spring?" he asked, sounding a little worried.

"He's going to give me away. He said he wouldn't miss it for anything. He wants to ride a horse while he's in Montana and eat steak, he said."

"So he isn't coming just to make sure I'm good enough for his goddaughter?"

She smiled over at her fiancé. "Oh, he's definitely doing that. But I wouldn't worry too much if I were you. He's the one who brought us together, so he only has himself to blame for the way it turned out."

DJ pulled her closer. "Thanks, I feel so much better." He grinned. "Have I told you how much I love you and that I can't wait to marry you?"

"I believe you have mentioned it." She matched his grin.

"You did save me, you know," he said quietly.

"The odds were against you and me, and yet you bet on me."

She cupped his handsome face in her hands. "I'd bet on you any day, DJ Diamond. I love you and I always will."

They heard their family calling to them. The barbecued ribs were ready.

"Hungry?" DJ asked.

"Starved," she said. He put his arm around her, and they headed back toward the Fourth of July picnic birthday party. "Ansley asked me what your favorite cake was. When I wouldn't tell her, she said, 'Fine. Lori will make my favorite then.' Wanna guess what it is?"

"Chocolate?" DJ asked with a grin.

"Chocolate."

"Did she mention that we are twins?" he joked as they joined the party. "You are aware that twins run in my family, right?"

"How else can we keep up with all these Colts otherwise?" Sadie said, and laughed. She couldn't wait to have babies with this cowboy. "In fact, I was thinking. After the party... I mean, it is your *birthday*."

* * * * *

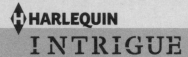
#2181 CONARD COUNTY: KILLER IN THE STORM
Conard County: The Next Generation • by Rachel Lee

For police deputy Artie Jackson, helping a handsome stranger stranded in a blizzard is a no-brainer. But Boyd Connor has his own demons and troubles. And possibly a connection to the stalker threats suddenly plaguing Artie...

#2182 MURDER IN TEXAS
The Cowboys of Cider Creek • by Barb Han

Dillen Bullard is only in town for one reason—to find out the truth behind his father's murder. Liz Hayes agrees that the circumstances are shady. But can Dillen trust his former nemesis to expose the culprit, or is Liz part of the cover-up?

#2183 SECRETS OF SILVERPEAK MINE
Eagle Mountain: Critical Response • by Cindi Myers

When search and rescue volunteer Caleb Garrison and forensic reconstructionist Danielle Priest team up to identify a murdered woman, they're swept into a web of secrets—and an attraction neither can deny. Then a case of mistaken identity threatens Danielle's safety and Caleb must risk everything to keep her safe.

#2184 MISTY HOLLOW MASSACRE
A Discovery Bay Novel • by Carol Ericson

Jed Swain served time for a crime he never committed. Now he dedicates his life to helping others find justice. Until his accuser's murder reunites him with Hannah Maddox, the woman he can't forget. And returns him to the small island where long-held secrets are about to be revealed...

#2185 ALWAYS WATCHING
Beaumont Brothers Justice • by Julie Anne Lindsey

Real estate agent Scarlet Wills is being hunted by someone she can't see but who knows her every move. Private investigator Austin Beaumont vows to keep her safe even as their attraction ignites. But when the stalker goes from escalating to unraveling, will Scarlet and Austin escape a dangerous trap?

#2186 HOMICIDE AT VINCENT VINEYARD
A West Coast Crime Story • by Denise N. Wheatley

As the newest police chief of Clemmington, California, Jake Love makes his first objective to solve the cold case murder of Vincent Vineyard's owner. His new girlfriend, Ella Bowman, is happy to help...until her dangerous ties to the Vincent family threaten her relationship with Jake, as well as her life.

HICNM1023

Get 3 FREE REWARDS!

We'll send you 2 FREE Books plus a FREE Mystery Gift.

FREE Value Over **$20**

Both the **Harlequin Intrigue®** and **Harlequin® Romantic Suspense** series feature compelling novels filled with heart-racing action-packed romance that will keep you on the edge of your seat.

HARLEQUIN
PLUS

Try the best multimedia subscription service for romance readers like you!

Read, Watch and Play.

Experience the easiest way to get the romance content you crave.

Start your **FREE TRIAL** at
www.harlequinplus.com/freetrial.